A STOR'

BY

KELLY POPE

To Sabrina
Keep smiling through the
good times and the
tougher times

Enjoy

Love Kelly Pope

Acknowledgements

Many thanks to everyone for all your
support in making this project possible

Andrew Murphy

Author of

The Quicksilver Report

Power Games

Assassins Dance

Matt Pope

Sarah Sutton

Shannon Roberts

Paul Jackson

About

A Story Of Fate was started when I was 17 years old. At the time I started this project I was in part time work, full time education and when I wasn't working or studying I was a full time carer for my grandmother.

I knew straight away this would not be completed quickly. Although I worked on it every day I sometimes could only manage 10 – 20 minutes.

It started life as a screenplay. I intended the screenplay to be a dark comedy about two individuals who were un-knowingly related and having such a bad day that you could not help but laugh at their misfortune.

After finally finishing it at 25 I naturally attempted to pitch it to various production companies around the UK. Unfortunately all that had agreed to read it were too small and unable to make it. A friend, Nick from Spearhead Films who had helped with printing and also read it said it could be done a lot cheaper by someone in America or another country. He suggested it would be good to turn it into a book that mirrored the screenplay. I stored the script away and created a back story leading to what I already had as the start of the film.

Whilst parts of the story may seem dark it is nothing but meaningless fiction. To this day I am still a fan of the A-Team and to a degree found myself sub consciously inspired by the idea of the good guys being renegades. It also contains my interest in Ninjutsu and Kenpo Karate.

Today I now live in South Devon and enjoy astronomy, martial arts, playing musical instruments and cross stitch. Under no circumstances will there be more than one sequel and A Story Of Fate 2: Tyler's Return will be dedicated to the memory of a great boss, friend and mentor who changed the direction of my life and always believed in me, David Vink.

Chapter 1

You very often hear it said that blood is thicker than water. This case is certainly no exception. Fights out of love for each other should only bring you closer. Once a bond is formed it can never be broken. Or can it? Regardless of any arguments that any couple naturally had, Mathew and Leandra, eventually, would always find a way to forgive each other. They had an unbreakable bond formed out of their undying love for each other. They trusted each other with their lives. They were a perfect couple like characters out of a fairy tale story.

It was on the first day of secondary school that Mathew and Leandra first met all those years ago. The school hall was full of nervous and excited adolescents meeting new people and waiting to be assigned their classes when they first laid eyes on each other from across the hall. For a brief moment, time seemed to stand still as they felt chills down their spines. The chemical reaction was instantaneous. Mathew nervously walked over to introduce himself. Everyone around them could tell straight away that they would one day end up together. They looked so good together. They were both shy at first and months went by before they even started talking to each other. In the meantime they smiled bashfully and their hearts pounded every time they met. They eventually became best of friends and quickly realised that they had quite a few things in common. Very soon after, Mathew and Leandra were officially known as an item. As fate would have it they would later grow to become soul mates.

Their relationship continued to grow even stronger as they carried on seeing each other after leaving school. In a lot of ways they were good for each other. It was obvious every time you saw them look at each other that they were truly in love. It was clear it was something that would never change which was just as well given the horrendous trials and tribulations that would befall them in their future. Mathew always took great pleasure in going out of his way to look after her and shower her with love, affection and gifts.

It made Leandra feel a little weird spending the evening of February 13th alone without even any phone contact from Mathew. Her melancholy mind raced as she wondered if he had lost interest in her and meant the end to their long running relationship. As more time went on with no contact, more sinister and distressing thoughts started racing through her mind. Was he ill or in some kind of danger? Was he cheating on her with another woman and had no intention of returning to her? With a book in one hand and a glass of wine in the other, Leandra submerged herself in a roasting hot bubble bath to help her relax before bed. She woke up on the morning of Valentine's Day to find her bedroom sprinkled in realistic looking foam rose petals, breakfast in bed and Mathew down on one knee with a ring, asking for her hand in marriage. She couldn't believe her eyes. 'Surprise. I love you Leandra, and I want to spend the rest of my life with you. Will you marry me?' He asked. She felt her eyes fill with tears of joy as she accepted his proposal. It was the best and most memorable Valentine's Day she would ever have. She even forgave him for keeping her in the dark and avoiding her the day before.

Both of their parents were ecstatic when Mathew and Leandra told them the news. Two weeks later all of their family and friends came to celebrate their engagement. They were lucky. Everyone in Mathew and

Leandra's family got on well together. They felt blessed as it wasn't the case for some of their friends. The church was packed, bells ringing, video camera at the ready. Mathew was so eager he was ready an hour before it was time to leave the house. The organ started playing. A nervous Mathew stood, frozen at the altar, and completely mesmerised by the heavenly sight of Leandra approaching in her long, white, very finely decorated wedding dress. The whole church was melted by their passionate kiss as they were pronounced husband and wife. It was the happiest day of Mathew and Leandra's life but, as it turned out not everyone was so happy for them.

Each of the three wealthiest relatives signed over one of their companies to Mathew and Leandra. This was to be a joint wedding gift to provide them with a strong and secure financial future for their life together. They loved their lives. They had their own roof over their heads, companies which they could work to thrive and generate secure finances and above all, love. Everything was perfect for a while but little did they know of the traumatising events that would happen in the years to come.

Not everything in the following years to come was bad. Mathew and Leandra were over the moon when she gave birth to their first child, a little boy who they named Mark. Life couldn't be more perfect. A few years later this joy was relived when she gave birth to their second child, this time being a beautiful girl who they named Lisa. Life was good, they had no financial issues and two healthy and happy children who knew they were deeply loved and receiving the best education that money could buy. Lisa and Mark were the typical brother and sister. They were often getting into fights with each other but just like their parents they would have a very strong bond between them. They would often watch them and chuckle with pride as it was like watching themselves to a degree, but in miniature. It was in Mark's nature that he was very protective over Lisa, just as Mathew was with Leandra (and obviously his children). He would never let anyone touch her or let her be in any danger at any time and he didn't care what it meant doing.

When you're a kid there's only so much you can do when danger strikes. Even though he was considered tough for his age everyone, especially kids have limitations. Threats on the family meant that they were having to constantly watch their back and everything happening around them on a day to day basis. It was a horrifying thing to live with and Leandra's greatest concern wasn't for herself or Mathew but how the whole situation may affect Lisa and Mark. Leandra was a firm believer that no child should live in fear, and here they were, her own flesh and blood being put through exactly that. Living in fear for her children's safety was eating away at her day by day. She found herself becoming more and more protective and strict with them. Another three months passed and everyone was finally starting to feel more relaxed. All had gone quiet. All their worst fears were beginning to fade, they hoped they could start to have a normal life again but little did they actually know how all that was about to go so very wrong. Everyone was hopeful that it was a one off scare and were totally unprepared and unsuspecting of the traumatic events that they would soon have to repeatedly endure.

The day started off the same as any normal Saturday morning, the sun was shining and everything was calm but it wasn't to stay that way. That afternoon Mark and Lisa had run into trouble on the way back from the local park near to their house. Hand in hand they raced to the safety of their home as quick as they could. Both Mark and Lisa had been that shaken and upset by the incident that happened on the way back that they had now become like rabbits in a set of headlights, going to great lengths to stay away from all the windows. The door handle moved. Young Mark stood in front, guarding Lisa, watching the door, his heart racing with fear. The door swung open. There were big sighs of relief as they realised it was their mother. They started to hyperventilate in panic as tears started streaming down their little faces.

Leandra took one look at them and flew over on her knees to try and comfort them. 'Mark, Lisa, what's wrong?' she asked as she hugged them and held them close trying to calm them down. Mark tried to stay calm as he explained that two men drove alongside them, trying to convince them to get in the car with them and kept watching them like a hawk before eventually driving off. He feared for their safety. He may have only been ten but he was already becoming a good judge of character. He didn't trust them, and he was right. 'Mathew, quick' yelled Leandra. She told Mathew what Mark had just told her as he held them close. A look of shock washed over his face at the thought of someone attempting to abduct his children. It was every parent's worst nightmare. Seeing his children upset made him feel sick in the stomach as his heart sank. Leandra was trying not to cry and attempting to hide how dreadfully worried she was. 'Oh Mathew, what are we going to do?' asked Leandra. He walked over and locked the front door and Leandra went to lock the back doors until she was stopped by Mark saying he had already done it. The incident was naturally taken very seriously.

As well as being a close friend of the family Jake Roberts was an officer in charge of the local police force. His oldest son David was in the same year at school with Mark, they were friends and got on well together. Within fifteen minutes of putting the phone down officer Jake Roberts and four other policemen arrived at the house. Mathew answered the door and let them in after cautiously identifying who they were. 'Sorry Jake, glad you could get here so quick, thanks' said Mathew.

'That's alright, not a problem' he said. 'Remember anytime you need me or anything just pick up the phone, you know how to reach me' he reassured him. Mathew nervously and silently smiled back with gratitude, granting them access to the house.

Mathew walked into the kitchen to check on Leandra as two of the policemen sat down with the kids. 'How are you feeling?' said Mathew. 'I'm so scared, oh Mathew, why can't it end? The poor kids are petrified, I can't handle it anymore' she replied as she burst into tears. He put his arms around her trying to reassure her. 'I try to keep it together in front of the kids' she added. 'I know, we'll get through it, I promise, I love you all so much' said Mathew. 'I love you too' replied Leandra. He put his arm around her as she wiped away her tears as they walked back to be with the kids trying to keep up a brave face in front of them.

The whole ordeal had clearly been too much for Lisa to try and handle and was taken to a different room to try and let Mark answer questions without any risk of distressing her further. Despite being so young he held it all together incredibly well. It was obvious to everyone how difficult it was for him and could tell he was trying to be brave whilst battling back tears. He answered every question in as much detail as possible not missing a thing no matter how little in case it helped to catch them. It was an event that any child, or adult for that matter would find extremely stressful to try and deal with.

'I was not gonna let them take her, no one touches my sister' said Mark staring vacantly and talking in monotone before distraughtly ending the interview in floods of tears in his father's arms. Everybody couldn't help but be really impressed with how Mark coped. 'You were exceptional, you did so well and everyone is proud of you' said one of the policemen who had knelt down next to him and held his hand. They were shocked how courageous and determined Mark was to assist in the making of an e-fit picture. 'I'm so proud of you, you've been so brave, well done' said Mathew as he hugged Mark. Mark burst into tears again. 'I'm scared daddy. I don't want anything to happen'. Mathew held him close, trying to reassure him and calm him down, trying desperately to make him feel safe. Everyone's heart went out to the whole family. Even the hardened policemen were now battling back tears watching Mark.

'OK you know what to do' said Jake. Two of the officers walked out. 'We'll let you know if we get anything' one said as they got in the car and drove off.

Leandra got started on cooking dinner whilst Mathew looked after the kids and carried on talking to Jake and the remaining police officers. Even though everyone had calmed down; deep down they were all experiencing that same gut feeling. The feeling that said that this was nowhere near over, that things were about to get worse in some way. Unfortunately they weren't over reacting. It would turn out to be the very cruel truth.

Leandra walked over to Mathew as the police were getting ready to leave. They told Mathew and Leandra they would keep them informed of anything that they came up with as they walked out the door. Afternoon quickly turned to evening, light turned to dark. Lisa watched out of the living room window as one of the police cars did another drive by in an attempt to deter anyone that might still be in the area from trying anything. A few times they even waved back or made funny faces to try and make Mark and Lisa laugh. Hours of looking and they still hadn't managed to catch the men or find any suspects who had earlier tried to get them into the car with them. They tried their upmost to stay calm. Everyone was convinced, even Mark and Lisa; that with the police driving past at such short intervals that they would be safe from any kind of immediate danger. Shortly after they drove past, a noise was heard outside. Mathew and

Leandra swiftly got the kids away from all the doors and windows just in case. Another louder, suspicious noise was heard. They felt sick at the realisation that their house was now surrounded.

Deafening banging was heard on the doors accompanied by various muffled voices, one of which Mark recognised from earlier that day. His heart sank as he took Lisa's hand. Mathew ran to the phone and attempted to raise the alarm. He got through to the station and started to speak but then got cut off. He knew at that point they had a very big problem. Whoever it was outside, was only seconds away from gaining entrance, the wires had been cut, all the phones were dead and they had absolutely no idea how long any help would be, if at all. There was no time to think of potential consequences when there was the distinct possibility that no one was coming to help them. The only care in the world now was protecting the children to the best of their abilities.

A few seconds later, Mark and Lisa ran away to hide as a group of men came flying through the door. They hoped that a neighbour will have heard some of the commotion and raise an alarm. That was a big if with living in an area where almost all of the houses had their own plot of land and slightly isolated. Mathew and Leandra tried as hard as possible to fight them off as Mark and Lisa darted into a bedroom, closing the door behind them. They prayed they wouldn't be found and for the safety of their parents who were putting their lives on the line to protect them.

They were over powered and greatly outnumbered. The kids meant everything to them and they were adamant that they weren't going down without a fight. Mark held hands with his sister. 'I promise, I'll never let anything happen, we'll never be apart' said Mark. 'I love you' replied Lisa as they hugged. Both of them were shaking as their adrenaline levels continued to rise. Mark's heart was once again racing faster than ever with fear as they heard people coming and suspected they were about to be found. His eye was drawn to a photograph of the pair of them which had been taken five days before. He picked up the photo and ripped it in half giving the section with him on to Lisa and he kept the half with her on. They quickly hid it away deep in their pockets just before one of the men from that afternoon appeared at the door.

Mark stood tall and jumped in front of Lisa. He felt slight chills as the adrenalin started surging even faster through his body. He realised in that moment that he was willing to die for her and gave no thought to his own actions. He gave the man a mighty push as he went to step forward. 'No one touches my sister' screamed Mark. There was absolutely nothing he could say to stop him attempting to snatch Lisa away. Mark was determined to protect her; and he knew he would have a hell of a tough fight on his hands. There was no time for fear, just bravery and determination. He tried not to show it but deep down he was petrified the whole time.

A few seconds later Mark and the man had sparked up a punch up as Lisa cowered in the corner trying to stay out of the way. Mark hit him with everything he could. There must have been a phenomenal amount of emotion running through Mark's system with the strength he was producing for his age and size. The chair fell apart as Mark smashed it over the man when he got chance between being pushed around. Unfortunately it wasn't enough to stop or deter him. The man very quickly realised that he was never going to get to Lisa until he got through Mark. 'Fine, no mercy you little brat' said the man as he started punching and kicking him repeatedly. Mark was constantly trying hard to fight back as the man used him as a punch bag. Lisa watched terrified as he continued to beat Mark into unconsciousness. He made sure there was no way he could wake up in time to stop him.

He wasn't moving. After passing Lisa to an accomplice the man pulled his gun and aimed it at Mark. The accomplice covered Lisa's mouth as she started screaming, looking back at Mark, convinced he was dead. He was just about to fire when he heard another voice say they had to leave immediately. He sighed as he ran out putting his gun away. Both Mathew and Leandra fought with everything they had but there was no one that could stop them taking Lisa.

Leandra let out a devastating scream in Mathew's arms as one of the two police cars chased the vehicles that had been seen fleeing from their house at high speed. They ran back inside the house frantically searching and shouting to Mark at the top of their voice. There was no answer. The thought had crossed her mind that he may have been taken as well. Leandra screamed hysterically and feared the worst as she spotted her son lying lifeless and bloody on the floor. Mathew and the policemen came running as fast as they could. One of the policemen radioed for an ambulance. Another cop knelt down next to Mark and checked his vital signs. She burst into tears as they were told he was still alive.

Leandra Knelt down emotionally by Mark's side and held his hand afraid to touch him in case it caused him pain. She kept talking to him trying everything to get a response but nothing worked. Still he remained lifeless.

Just then the ambulance arrived at the house. They leapt out with the stretcher and ran inside as the policeman explained about Mark. They both froze for a brief second totally shell shocked as they burst through the door. Nothing could have prepared them for the sight of Mark. It was abundantly clear that someone didn't want him to live. Leandra stood up to make way for the paramedics. For the two paramedics involved it was an incident that would haunt them forever. They were sickened to think how this little helpless boy had suffered at the hands of another individual. Their stomachs churned. In all their years in the service they had never seen a more brutal attack on anyone, least of all a young, defenceless child. Mathew put his arms around Leandra and watched as Mark was being hooked up to heart monitors and oxygen as he was being carefully placed on the stretcher.

They ran out and got him into the ambulance as fast as they could. One of the policemen and Leandra went with Mark. Mathew and the other policemen said they would catch up with them later. They drove off with the lights flashing and sirens blaring. Leandra was an absolute wreck as Mark fell into cardiac arrest in the ambulance. She thanked the shaken paramedic repeatedly as they managed to get a heartbeat to return. At casualty doctors were at the ready.

He was admitted straight away and given a private room with a police guard. One of the biggest concerns for everyone was the fact that after all this time Mark had not once even vaguely managed to regain consciousness or respond to any questions. Intensive care doctors had become concerned at the possibility that he might be seriously brain damaged or worse have suffered brain death. They battled extensively throughout the night to keep him alive.

Mark was in very bad shape. They were doing everything they could for him and kept his parents constantly updated. No one knew what would happen over the next few hours; only that for Mark they were critical. No one could give them an answer. Anything could happen; he could start to show signs of waking up or not make it through another night. Mark had been so severely beaten that doctors placed his chances of survival at no more than about thirty five percent.

It was the worst day of their lives. No one knew how Mark would be, their daughter was gone, no contact or ransom from anyone had been received, not even a sighting. Their home and lives were destroyed and thrown into total chaos.

Mathew and Leandra tightly held each other close as they walked through the doors of intensive care filled with dread and not knowing what to expect. Mark was black and blue with cuts, fractures and a few inflammations but they were overwhelmed with relief when they were told that his condition appeared to show signs of stabilizing. Although he had not woken up this was an extremely good sign. The doctors believed that their efforts had paid off by managing to raise his chances of living by five percent. Mark was in no way out of danger. They still had a lot more tests to run and they were well aware that his condition could deteriorate at any moment. The senior consultant ordered his exhausted staff to hide the possibility that Mark still may die from his parents.

Jake and his men were working hard alongside the forensic team to try and catch the assailants responsible but struggled to have any success at all. If such an unlikely thing as inside help was used it was almost impossible to positively identify who. Later that day, Mathew and Leandra faced cameras to make an emotional appeal to the culprits and to the general public for any kind of information that may help to get Lisa back. It was sent out on an international broadcast trying to cover every possibility. Posters would be found literally anywhere in the world. They could try no harder but she appeared to have dropped off the face of the earth, leaving them to fear that she had already been murdered.

Three weeks later Mathew and Leandra received a message they didn't expect, they couldn't believe it when the doctor said he had good news. They rushed out gathering pyjamas as they had been asked to. They were so excited and raced to the hospital as soon as they could. Their nerves were on overload.

Mathew and Leandra approached the nurse's station. One of the nurses put down the phone and told them there was a nurse with Mark and the doctor would come along as soon as possible. Leandra walked over and held his hand. 'How's he doing?' asked Mathew. 'I know it probably doesn't seem like it but he's started responding really well to treatment but that's for the doctor to discuss with you I can't really tell you anything for certain' replied the nurse. The nurse was just a nurse and always getting into a lot of trouble for getting a diagnosis wrong and now on a final warning but they liked the sound of it and hoped it was right. A few minutes later the senior consultant walked through the door and greeted Mathew and Leandra. The nurse took Mark's pyjamas as they walked out to the office to talk.

They closed the door and sat down. He told them that his recent tests had shown that he had no brain damage and would regain perfect sight again. 'I'm very sorry to say that nothing's going to happen quickly but I feel fairly positive that eventually he will make a full recovery' said the consultant. Mathew hugged Leandra as she cried in relief. The consultant told them to talk to him to aid recovery after they spotted him very slowly waking up, slipping in and out of consciousness for a few seconds at a time once or twice that day. They were over joyed. Mark was going to live.

It was a sign of hope that maybe, just maybe in time they'll be able to get their life back, but they knew that this could never be a possibility without their beloved daughter and sister. Without getting Lisa back their lives could never really be complete no matter how hard they tried.

They took it in turns to ensure one of them was at his side to talk to him and comfort him as much as possible often spending on average sixteen hours a day at his bed side. They took some comfort from the excellent standard of care that their delicate child was receiving. He was kept fed and hydrated via drip, regular oxygen whenever he needed it and constantly, gently rotated him to stop him getting any bedsores. After two months had passed; they slept heavy through pure exhaustion, during which, little did they know of the miraculous improvement that Mark was making.

A refreshed Mathew and Leandra turned up at the hospital. Their nerves tried to fight their way out of their bodies and they held hands tightly as their hearts sank. They feared the worst as they were approaching his room to find it being cleaned out and a nurse approaching them. The nurse stopped them and told them the good news that Mark had regained consciousness for longer periods of time and had just been moved to a private room on a normal ward. They were filled with relief to hear that he no longer needed to be in intensive care.

Mathew and Leandra found their way to the new ward. Everyone's faces lit up with joy and surprise as they walked in and found Mark sat up in the bed, high on painkillers and sedatives with an oxygen mask. For the first time in months they could now see their son awake and responsive. 'Mum, dad' Mark weakly called out. They walked over and hugged and kissed him gently. 'I'm so glad you're alright' said Mathew. Oh Mark my baby' said Leandra emotionally holding his hand, smiling immensely.

Regardless of how badly he was beaten up, Mark was still able to recall everything that happened in great detail. It was a traumatic event that would haunt him for a very long time, longer than even he could ever have imagined. 'What happened to Lisa? Where is she?' Mark asked. It was a day they were dreading. They tried to keep it together whilst Mathew had to try and find a way to break the news to Mark that the ambush was successful and his sister had been abducted. Mark was heartbroken and felt consumed with guilt. Leandra gently put her arms around Mark as he burst into tears. 'I'm really sorry, I tried so hard to stop them, Lisa' Mark cried. 'Mark, it's OK, I know, it's not your fault, you did everything you could, don't do that no one blames you, it's OK, I know, I know, I love you' replied Leandra as they both hugged and kissed him. Everyone in the town was in total disbelief over everything that the family had recently been through. Mark's hospital room was full of gifts, flowers and get well soon cards that people in pretty much the entire area had sent. He appreciated and liked everything that he received; it helped to try and lift his spirits a little. Mark would be guaranteed to get at least one visitor a day, even if he wasn't conscious at the time to be aware of it. His parents and grandparents often took it in turns to be with him during the time in hospital. Jake Roberts would be the first non-family member to visit Mark and often popped in to see how he was doing, sometimes business, sometimes pleasure. He ensured that an officer remained on guard outside his room at all times. They were hand-picked. Jake was not prepared to take any chances.

Mark missed Lisa so much. He couldn't bare the thought of not getting her back and still there was no sign of her possible return. He was given regular sessions with a child trauma counselling specialist to try and help him cope with his ordeal. All that time in hospital had given Mark plenty of time to think. He'd already decided on the option to repeat the school year as the end of the current school year was rapidly approaching. Although he kept it from everyone at the time, Mark was adamant that he would dedicate his life to finding her, study hard and learn as many skills as possible in case it may one day help him track his sister down. He loved her so much. He was determined he would do literally anything he could no matter how extreme to help him succeed. It was a concept that had many people very concerned about his mental well-being, especially at such a young age.

Four and a half months had passed and Mark's continued improvement meant that even though he would be making regular return visits for further tests and check-ups he was finally ready to be going home. He looked forward to a change of surroundings and having his parents under the same roof at night.

Mathew had already taken almost all of his gifts home during the week. He took as much as he could to the car whilst Leandra picked up a few remaining things with Mark and said goodbye and thanks to all the hospital staff who worked so hard to save his life. They were eternally grateful to everyone who took such good care of him. He was going home just in time for his eleventh birthday.

Mark refused to give up hope that he would one day be reunited with his little sister and have a new life with each other. It didn't matter what he was doing or where he was he would never give up scanning his surroundings in case he spotted her.

The events that happened that night would traumatise him for a very long time to come. He found it immensely challenging, returning home to try and carry on with his life. Every night for years he was haunted by nightmares. Some of them containing flashbacks of the ambush and others of his memories he had of Lisa in his life. He was frightfully desperate and determined with little regard for his own safety. Lisa's memory was something no one could ever forget. Three times a year, Mark would go to a local church to light a candle and prey for her return. It was always on the exact same date; on the date of the ambush when she was taken, her birthday and Christmas day. These were the most difficult and upsetting dates for the whole family. In all the years, he never missed any of the three dates. He hoped his prayers would one day be answered.

The events that happened to Mark and his family were things that no family should ever have to endure. The devastation was enough to drive anyone off the rails. No one could predict what it would do to Mark. It was down to fate to determine how Mark would turn out, what kind of man he would grow into and what would happen in the future, if there was one.

The years flew by and Mark was no longer a kid but now a teenager. With no contact no one had a clue where Lisa was or even if she was dead or alive. He often reflected on his earlier years. It broke his heart to think back on his childhood and all the things that they should have faced together, instead of the lonely time he sometimes faced with Lisa missing from his life.

Mark became one of the most intelligent people you could meet. He studied so hard both at home and when he was in school and was top of his class the whole time. He could always surprise you with the things he knew and the skills he was capable of. Mark could have had any job he liked but there was only ever one thing on his mind. Lisa.

Over the years Mark learnt to trust his instinct. He went walking alone after another unsuccessful investigation into finding Lisa but he couldn't shake the feeling that he had company. He looked around highly suspicious that someone was watching him; thinking that he was over reacting from stress. Mark had no idea what would happen next as he sat down with his head in his hands trying to remain calm.

He sat overlooking the sea when something caught his eye making him look over his shoulder. His nerves jumped and he froze as he looked back to the right and found an envelope with his name on. He slowly picked up the note which seemed to appear out of nowhere. He had no idea who gave him the note or how they knew his name. He was shaken. He felt a cold chill go down his spine as he felt the hairs on the back of his neck stand up.

He looked around but couldn't figure out who might have given it to him. Little did he know that the person responsible for leaving the note had silently slipped away and was now suspended off the edge, safely hidden from sight. He stood up and headed for the first quiet place he could find to be able to read the note in private totally unaware that his every move was still being watched. The man on the ledge returned to solid ground after being told through an ear piece that the coast was clear and there was no chance of being discovered by Mark.

He opened the envelope and started to nervously read the cryptic note he found inside that read:

'Mark, We've been watching you,

We know what you are doing, we understand.

You have great potential for the future but the future is nothing without family.

We may be able to help you like no one else ever could'

These were words that certainly struck a nerve for Mark who was so desperate to find her. Also in the note was a time and place to meet later that day, alone.

Mark went home. He paced around the house before going to his room. He couldn't get the words he read in the note out of his head. He laid on his bed thinking about everything, the note and the lengths he would go to even if it meant putting his own life at risk. He tried to dispel the feeling that it all sounded too good to be true. Even if it was too good to be true it was something he wanted more than life itself.

Leandra appeared at the door and saw how upset Mark was. She walked over and sat down next to him on the bed. 'Who was on the phone?' he asked. The look on his mother's face said it all. 'Same as last time?' asked Mark. 'Nothing new' Leandra replied shaking her head. Every now and again someone would ring up out of the blue and claim they knew where to find Lisa and sometimes, especially recently saying they would kill her. It made them sick. They never knew how much truth there was in it or when someone was going to ring up to taunt them.

He felt so confused, it was depressing, the whole situation tore him up inside. His parents were fantastic; they were the best a child could hope for. He knew he could always discuss anything and never felt he had to keep any kind of secrets no matter what they were about.

Despite his efforts to hide his emotions he clearly looked scared. Leandra placed her hands on his arms. 'Whatever it is, it doesn't matter, trust me, there's nothing you can't tell me' Leandra told him. 'I shouldn't be telling anyone' said Mark almost in tears. 'You can tell me' pushed Leandra. Mark sat up and gave Leandra the note to read telling her how most of the day he hadn't been able to shake the feeling that he was being watched yet oddly didn't feel threatened. He felt so confused.

His parents were just as eager as Mark to find Lisa. Leandra was scared but very supportive of Mark as long as he was careful and didn't try and blindly run into anything that he may later regret. 'You're the best mum in the world' said Mark as they hugged. Part of her knew he would do it anyway but they had a great relationship and she was desperate for it to stay that way even if it tore her up inside or she didn't agree or fully approve. She had already lost a daughter, the last thing she wanted to do was drive her son away. He was determined to do what the note said. He was way too scared to let it pass in case it was a decision that would later work to his benefit in some way.

'Please be careful' said Leandra as Mark walked out the door. She put on a brave face then cried as the door shut and he was out of sight. He went to the location given in the note and waited. His heart was pounding. It was one of the most isolated spots in the entire area. He felt so nervous in case it was some kind of cruel prank or attempt on his life but it was still a risk that he was willing to take.

He once again had a feeling he was being followed by someone. He acted swiftly as he turned around in time to block a punch from a large built man about to jump on him. The man smiled as he asked 'are you Mark?' Mark nodded and replied he was without letting his guard down. They stood down. 'Let's walk' said the man. They walked off talking. The man apologised for going at Mark the way he did telling him it was part of a test. 'You did well' he said as they shook hands and introduced himself as Rob. 'Thanks I guess' replied Mark trying not to shake and maintain a calm and confident persona and trying to steady his breathing.

Rob stopped and stood looking at Mark. He found Mark's reactions impressive. 'Our group is built on trust, relax, you can trust me' said Rob. Seconds later a black van with blacked out windows pulled up. They approached the van. The side door swung open. The vans interior was more like a minibus than a van. Mark and Rob climbed in as one of the men closed the door behind them.

Mark didn't beat around the bush as he directly came straight out and asked them if it was a cruel prank or if it's true what was written in the note. 'For real' said one of the men. He felt vague hope as they told him they wanted to try and help him find his sister. He was grateful but couldn't understand why. A small part of him doubted that they would be able to shed some light when everyone else to date had failed. Mark started to get emotional as he told them every detail he could from the night she was taken and all the things that had happened since.

He knew they wanted to help and became strangely convinced that they could but he never had any idea that they were interested in recruiting him into their organisation. 'We have been watching you for some time, you have great potential' said the man sat behind the wheel. They went on to explain to Mark about who they were. He was speechless and felt overwhelmed with intimidation as he was told that they were all part of a unique underground military group. In a lot of ways this group was very different from others. They consisted of people from many different occupations such as accountants, doctors, cops, literally anyone. They came from all sorts of backgrounds and situations, on the run, set up, faked their own deaths, protecting and searching for people. Renegades.

These men were fearless and ruthless. They were highly unpopular with other military groups such as the army. They were renowned for completing missions before the army could start or even taking on missions that no one else would. Their strong point was the fact that every single person taught everyone every little thing they knew even down to bombs and explosives which made them lethal.

The man behind the wheel warned Mark never to attempt to expose any members or bring their group down as it would result in his death. They were famed and feared for sticking to their word and carrying out everything they said. If they said you would be killed then that's exactly what would happen make no doubt about it. Too much was at stake and exposure would mean endangering the lives of many non-members as well. They considered themselves like a family.

'Don't worry, you don't have to make a decision about that right this second' said Jason who was 6'4, medium build and full of muscle. Mark breathed a sigh of relief. They gave Mark a lift home so that Mathew and Leandra wouldn't worry. Mark was instructed to meet back up with them four days later for an update. No one else had any luck, he was curious to find out what, if anything they could come up with. He wanted desperately to believe that they could help.

Mathew and Leandra watched as they pulled up. They acted as normal as possible. 'Hi Mark' shouted Leandra as she waved. 'Hi mum' replied Mark. She walked over and put her arms around him as they waved at the van. 'See ya' said Mark as they waved and replied. They watched feigning a cheerful disposition as the van door slammed shut. Mark and Leandra walked back inside the house as the van drove off.

'Are you alright? I've been worried sick about you' said Leandra as they hugged. 'Yeah, I'm fine' replied Mark with a vague look on his face. He couldn't believe what was happening, the meeting had yet to sink in. This was something he would definitely have to tell his parents and hope they would understand, if at all possible. How could he tell them? He was so desperately eager he was actually considering joining them but he was also way too scared to do anything to double cross them in any way. It was a heavy situation, one of the hardest decisions he would ever have to make.

Mathew and Leandra questioned Mark about what happened and how it went. He told them about them wanting him to join and how they were sure they could help find Lisa but Mathew and Leandra's big concern was losing Mark, and as well as with Lisa not knowing vital things such as where they are, are they alright?, or even more importantly if they were alive.

Mark was full of mixed thoughts and emotions, so much so that it was actually frightening. He knew it was a big decision and they'd be expecting an answer very soon.

That night Mark relived the nightmare of his sister's abduction in great detail in his dreams. He woke up in a sweat, crying and shaking, in shock. He felt suffocated in pain as the devastating memories flooded back. The dream felt as real as it did the first time round. It seemed like it had only happened literally the night before. Mark had always been haunted by memories of the past and since the dream, had reawakened during the day making him feel like he was losing his grip on reality. The flashbacks he was getting during the day were increasing in regularity as the time went by. They were the same flashbacks that happened for years after returning home from hospital. Deep down he knew that the trauma would never subside until he was able to bring the individuals responsible to justice whether it be legal or not.

The time had come to meet again. Today would be the day he had waited for all his life – an answer, answers of any kind, definitely better than none he thought to himself. All the way to the meeting point his stomach was turning, nerves were building, he had no idea what to expect. Jason watched as Mark approached. It was blatantly obvious to them how frightened and uncomfortable he was and yet they remained understanding. Jason was completely calm and stood tall and mighty like a soldier or professional bodyguard.

They climbed into the van to talk in private. The moment of truth had come – did they have anything? He wasn't expecting anything. Mark was pleasantly surprised. He was told that the person who abducted Lisa was a man known by the name of Joshua, a corrupt boxer who worked for a notorious crime lord who wanted the companies that his parents owned signed over to them to use as fronts to run unsuspecting illegal operations. Rob held up a photo. 'That's him' Mark confirmed.

It brought back chilling memories to see a picture of the man who tried to kill him all those years ago. One of his first questions was about Lisa. He was told there was no definite but she was most likely still alive wherever she was. Even though they had found out who was definitely behind it there was nothing he could do as there was little or none that could currently be used as solid proof. But, at least now he knew, he had somewhere to start. Either way it was still a most welcomed step forward.

This was the most anyone had ever been able to give him. He couldn't believe it. These guys were amazing whoever they were. He thought back on the previous meeting and everything that had happened. He looked around at everyone. The question he was about to ask was one he felt he had to just in case, whatever the answer, it was also one that delighted them all. He took a deep breath and asked them how and what would happen to him if he did join them. They all smiled briefly. Jason introduced the rest of the guys. 'Me and Rob you already know, this is Ethan and Tyler' he said as he pointed to each one accordingly. They told him he would be given full training before doing anything vaguely dangerous. 'Don't worry. If you're not completely ready then I'll hold you back and you won't be doing it' said Tyler. Even though Tyler was smiling as he said it, Mark found something in his eyes, something about him, extremely intimidating. Even his own friends appeared to be scared of him yet he couldn't figure out why.

Tyler was the guy who would be in charge of training up Mark and deciding whether or not he was capable and ready to participate in the next mission whatever it may be. The only way you could describe Tyler would be lethal. He was a tall and big built guy, (all you could see of him was solid visible muscle all over his body), martial arts instructor of a variety of styles, and an explosives and weapons expert with precision aim. He had also been diagnosed with hyperactivity and a photographic memory at a very young age which as you can imagine sometimes gave his parents quite a trying experience as he was growing up.

He was the founder and very well-liked and respected in the group; that much was abundantly clear. He often appeared to remain calm but in a split second could always display explosive energy; a live wire in any situation, a great guy but you would have to be careful as he was sometimes a little trigger happy. Either way Tyler would probably be the last person on earth that anyone would ever want to get on the wrong side of; especially if they placed any kind of value on their life.

When it came to missions and training the final decision was always made by Tyler. Even if they were unarmed they usually wore some kind of body armour. He was also assured that if it ever became necessary his family would be well protected should any cause for concern arise.

These words brought Mark some comfort. He was inclined to believe that they would. They told him that a man named John would secretly be able to protect his family. John, now a high ranking police chief had at one point been a member of their group. He left but often came back to help or ask for help. John was a young man at the time. He was a police officer, he joined after being set up and had false allegations made against him. He was one of the very early members of the group. He left after they helped him get a clean slate. He always says they found him just in time and he felt he couldn't be thankful enough for what they did for him.

Time had come for Mark to be heading back. He was told by Jason that the next time they would meet would be two weeks later. Tyler added that he would be expected to give an answer by then.

It was a very big decision to make. Mark and his parents spent a lot of time together over the next fortnight. He sat down and told them what they said. Obviously they weren't over keen on the idea but as always they remained supportive. It was a big risk and a trail of heartache and pain ahead but worth it if it meant that they may one day get both of their children back and have a real life which the thought of deep down broke their hearts. Mark had already decided that he would agree to join them.

The two weeks were up, today would be the day he would give them his answer. Mark decided to try and sneak up on them from a different direction to try and impress them and see how close he could get before they saw him coming. Everyone looked at Tyler bemused as he started giggling and laughing. He was very alert and had sharp eyes. He pointed out Mark. Tyler had spotted Mark's attempt but was amused with his efforts. They couldn't wait to hear his answer even though they had a feeling they already knew what it was. All arrangements were made depending on their individual situation prior to joining. Under the circumstances Tyler decided it would be best if Mark faked his death. He had a few ideas. Mark had no idea what to do. He just left it to Ethan, Jason and Tyler to arrange as Rob had told him to. He knew all along that this would be a temporary thing and they would one day when the time was right be able to prove he was alive. They instantly decided that it would be in some kind of accident. At the end of the day they did a great job. With no sign of a body and just vanishing off the face of the earth people would have no choice but to assume he must be dead. It seemed the plan had worked. People were beginning to back off.

After the big day Mark was taken straight to meet the other members of the military group. It was an unforgettable day. He felt rather awkward at times, starting a whole new kind of life with the rest of the world thinking he was dead. He was about to leave everyone and everything he knew behind and embark on a whole new adventure that would ultimately make or break him. Understandably as it would for anyone it was extremely overwhelming. He learnt how they worked and they started training him to fight and teaching him the basics of any kind of thing, except for explosives, a little risky for only his first week.

One of the first things that Mark realised was how well respected yet feared Tyler was. No one, even the people that had been accused of murder, would ever dare to answer back or question his judgement.

That evening was to be an eye opener for Mark when he and Tyler and some of the other guys went out. A mass punch up broke out on the other side of the room which led to someone making the deadly mistake of starting on Tyler. He was lethal, even knocking people out with only one strike. Mark stood and watched totally gob smacked as Tyler took down multiple assailants as big as him, rarely getting hit and barely breaking a sweat. Now he would officially be one of the gang so to speak. They were scared to death of him and he understood why. He was the real McCoy as they say; deadly.

Mark felt sure that if he worked very hard he could one day maybe be anywhere near as good as him. He became very fond and impressed with Mark's efforts; he was perfect, an amazing recruit and a very fast learner. He was right all along in saying that he had great potential. He continued to push him harder and harder when instructing him.

After a while Mark's death was no longer fooling Joshua and his associates as much as it should have. It was good whilst it lasted as it allowed him to learn vital new skills. Things had started to back fire. Mark had discovered they were starting to go after Lisa again wherever she may be and John had informed him that the tormenting phone calls to his parents had started up again. He decided the time had come to start plans to make a shocking re-appearance.

After endless hours of thought Mark had devised a plan. Part of the plan involved holding up a bank, swapping between three different getaway vehicles, making him impossible to trace, with the first bank hostage he could grab and use them as a bargaining chip. The bank manager was also due a bonus, if he kept his mouth shut he would get some of the money back but if he took matters further he would never see a penny of it and be immediately terminated to protect the group. As you can imagine they had excellent powers of persuasion.

It was time he was alive. Time he got his life back. Time he got his sister back.

Chapter 2

A lot of time had passed since the events that were eating him up inside took place. Mark was no longer a kid or a teenager but a young man, so many dramatic and unique life changes he had experienced. He had lost his sister and joined an underground military group from which he had learnt so much of what made him the man he was today.

Whenever Mark could, without putting anyone at any risk, he would always go and visit his aunt and uncle who lived in a very secluded luxury log cabin surrounded by woodland and its own lake running through their land. Understandably over the years Mark had become really depressed at working hard yet failing to get to the bottom of what happened to his sister and never seeing his parents as a result of faking his death to protect everyone he loved all those years ago. His uncle had proof that he was still alive and although he never saw them, his parents always knew that the mysterious gifts that turned up throughout the year was from their beloved son. They found it rather comforting because they knew it meant he was still alive and well, somewhere.

Mark and his uncle sat in the back garden talking about how much he missed Lisa. Although he was only a small boy there was nothing more he could have done, after all he did nearly die that day; he blamed himself for what had happened. He realised that he had been unable to move on and still carried unworthy guilt. His uncle's heart started racing as Mark told him that no matter how long it took, whether dead or alive he was determined he was going to find her and get his family back on its feet. He had faith in Mark but wasn't entirely convinced that despite his best efforts he would achieve his goal and it horrified his aunt and uncle. Getting to the truth and finding her would be like finding a needle in a field crammed full of haystacks. Mark pulled out the ripped in half photograph from when he was a kid. Every time he looked at it he had a flashback of ripping it in half just before she was snatched. Wherever she was she would have a picture of him on it. Mark told his uncle how it had never left his side.

Although they hid it rather well they were becoming worried sick about him and quite alarmed as he was still as devastated as if it had happened only yesterday. They knew and expected it to traumatise him and never expected him to ever forget his sister but it was at that point that they realised the ordeal had been ruling and shaping his entire life. 'Hold on, I'm coming, I promise' he said as he looked at the photo smiling. Secretly it sent shivers down his uncle's spine, he tried to maintain a calm and composed exterior in the presence of Mark. He struggled to find any tactful words that could comfort him so just placed his hands sympathetically on his shoulders.

Although Mark didn't know it yet Lisa was still alive. The upbringing she had after she was snatched meant that all and any memory of her life before had been buried deep inside her mind. Often as Lisa slept she found herself haunted by a flashback of the final words of an older woman with whom she grew up around. 'Somewhere out there your big brother has the other half of this photograph. He always has and will love you. I tried to protect you the best I could. Please forgive me. I am so sorry for everything that you have been through and what you must now face. Now you know this much you must secretly find him. As long as you're on your own your life is in danger, his name is...' Lisa sat in shock at what she had just learnt about herself. She never knew that she had a brother. The woman passed away before she could tell her his name. She had no idea what to do or who to trust. She couldn't risk or afford to hire a private detective and she had almost nothing to go on. All she had was a picture of her big brother as a young boy, even the background couldn't supply her with anything to go on as it was set against a blank wall. It was a lot to take in.

As sure as the woman had warned, it wasn't long before disturbing things started to happen. Lisa was sure that she wasn't paranoid or over reacting when there seemed to be a lot of regular near miss incidents happening. Incidents of attempted murder that could be made to look like an accident and it chilled her to the bone. She struggled intensely with the feeling of having to be constantly looking over her shoulder but something inside her was telling her to keep fighting through it all even though she had made no progress and the incidents were becoming almost as regular as clockwork.

Mark was on edge with the amount of adrenaline pumping through his body and stood nervously getting ready to do what he felt was necessary for implementing the first part of his plan and concentrated on remaining focused on his final goals.

He stood in front of the mirror clean shaven and well-groomed in black trousers loading a gun. He slipped a loose shirt over his prominently visible chest and arm muscles followed by a smart matching jacket. After getting dressed he calmly went into the living room and concealed the gun at waste height and a large survival knife on his leg. He was almost ready to go. He picked up different sets of keys and applied a fake moustache. The addition of a fake moustache dramatically changed his persona. Not only did he look a lot older but also like pure evil.

Chapter 3

Lisa left the house and headed off down the street. She had only been walking for about fifteen minutes and was stood on the path when she noticed a car screech round the corner approaching at great speed. She had a feeling that she knew what was about to happen as she watched it approaching. Her heart started racing the closer it got. She dove out of the way just avoiding being hit as it sped up and on to the path. It left her feeling shocked, winded and bruised as she pulled herself together and clambered to her feet. She had a feeling it was going to be another bad day ahead but could never have imagined just how bad and how emotional the rest of the day was about to become. Little did she know that today would turn out to be both the worst and the best day of her life.

Mark pulled up at a local bank shortly after opening, while the town would still be very quiet driving a very old car with no front or back number plates and casually entered the bank. A few seconds later Lisa felt like her head had been violently wrenched off her body as she felt herself struggling for air as Mark pulled out a gun, throwing his powerful built arm around her neck and shouting orders in a fake accent.

The thought instantly crossed her mind that this could be the day that her quest would end. She mentally started preparing herself for the worst, the moment he inevitably pulled the trigger. She could tell whoever he was, he was no opportunist; he meant business. She hadn't seen his face and all she knew was that he sounded calm, forceful and had a loaded gun. It quickly became clear that escape would be neon impossible. She was filled with fear as she felt the gun pressed firmly against her head and gasped desperately for air whilst unsuccessfully trying to loosen his grip on her throat. She tried to scream but physically couldn't. She was no match for him. She felt her life starting to drift away as she struggled to get away.

He threw a bag to the clerks. Despite her best efforts there was nothing she could do, he was far too strong. 'Try anything, I'll kill her you got it' he said with the gun against her head ready to fire. 'Her fate is in your hands' he said as they took it in turns to empty the money into the bag. Mark ordered everyone to lie face down on the floor. After moving to collect the money they started backing out.

They exited the bank and he forced her into the passenger seat of the car. Lisa had become very disorientated from the lack of air. He ran round and jumped in the driver's seat as she was trying to recover enough to figure out where she was and what was going on. As soon as she had, she made a frantic attempt to escape from the car. He crushed her against the seat as he leant across and shut the door again. She screamed as he slammed his fist down locking it.

'What do you think you're doing? Don't even think about it!' he said as he held her by the throat. She fought as hard as she could to try and rip his large hand away. She tried unsuccessfully to make a sound. Her throat and neck was on fire as he tightened his grip the more she tried to fight. Tears streamed down her face as she struggled to breathe whilst his sinister facial expression remained completely unchanged.

She was terrified and just wished her mysterious big brother would swoop in and rescue her, or anyone for that matter. As she suspected, the town was deserted with the exception of the other people in the bank and no one came. No one would even know what type of car they were in.

'The only way you're getting away is over my dead body you got that' he said as Lisa grimaced at the pain caused by the cold point of the gun crushing her ribs. He removed his hand from her throat and put the gun away as he started the car and drove off fast. She screamed and covered her face as they swerved to miss another car. 'Don't bother; no-one is following us' said Mark as Lisa looked out the back window as the car left the town. Her heart sank as Mark let out a laugh refusing as she tried to beg him to release her.

For both Mark and Lisa, in many ways the day was about to only go from bad to worse as the car broke down whilst driving through woodland and grinded to a halt. Mark gave her an evil look. 'Don't even, not a word' he said after being provoked by Lisa with the comment 'great car'.

As soon as she saw the look in his eyes she knew she should never had said it. It was a comment that could have got her killed. The car wouldn't start again.

He removed his seat belt and the keys from the ignition and removed the fake moustache. She was shocked at how different he looked as she had the first glance of what her captor actually looked like. Lisa slowly and cautiously took her seat belt off. Mark walked round telling her to get out as he opened the door. She felt a brief ray of hope as she thought for a moment she was going to be released and tried to run off.

She was in sudden paralytic agony as Mark quickly grabbed her roughly refusing to let go of her arm. 'You're coming with me' he said as he carried on walking with Lisa putting up a fight unsuccessfully. His strength was remarkable. Using his military knowledge he made a conscious effort to make sure some of the hold dug into a pressure point allowing him to inflict a lot more pain than just randomly grabbing her arm. It didn't matter what she tried she just couldn't break free from his iron grip. The more she tried to fight with him the more he increased the grip on the pressure point just above her elbow. It was hopeless. Eventually they arrived at a slightly newer car with blacked out plates and got in and drove off.

After about a forty minute drive they arrived at a house and pulled into the garage. Mark hit the remote control closing the garage door behind them. He waited for the door to be securely shut before he went round and dragged Lisa out of the car. She struggled and screamed as he locked her in an empty room connected to the garage with bars on all the windows. No way out.

She panicked, banging on the door and swearing at him for a while. No one came. She sat down against the wall on the floor crying. She had no idea what was going to happen to her. She felt so alone. She pulled out the photo from her pocket so that she could potentially have one last look at it. She felt consumed with guilt that they would probably never meet.

After collecting some things and getting changed into more comfortable clothing such as jeans and trainers he returned to the garage and unlocked the door. He flew in and roughly grabbed her by the hair. She screamed as he forced her into the car and drove off into the middle of nowhere. She thought he was going to kill her. If not yet, soon.

Neither of them could believe it when they were forced to start walking again as the car over heated. Mark got very snappy with her as she tried once again to convince him to let her go. It was by now clear that this was never going to happen. It had become apparent that he was never going to release her; all she could do now was wait and plunder her fate.

Chapter 4

Lisa and Mark eventually arrived at a large luxury camper van. 'Great. I'm starving' he said as he looked at Lisa and looked at the van smiling.

Mark had always loved his camper. It brought back both fond and unusual memories for him. Inside, they sat at the table opposite each other eating and drinking.

Mark had locked every door and window and closed all the curtains, holding her at gun point facing a panel with her hands behind her head before they began. He pulled out the knife that was strapped to his lower leg and placed it on the table next to him. She felt frozen and nauseous. It took her by surprise as she hadn't realised he had more concealed weapons.

Mark could tell by her very subtle actions that she was making an attempt to tactfully move the curtain as a vehicle was heard approaching from an unknown direction. She felt disorientated when her world spun as he gave her a vicious back hander across the face as punishment for trying to peak out of the curtain. He quickly grabbed her clothing and his knife and held the large blade firmly in to her throat. She was silent and unable to get any words out even if she wanted to. She froze in fear with tears streaming down her face. 'Disobey me again I'll cut your throat' he sternly warned. He laid the knife back down on the table next to him. They both drank. She was shaking as she held the cup against her face in an attempt to calm the fiery stinging sensation that he had left her with. For the first time since their chance encounter they exchanged names.

Lisa didn't know what to think when she was told that if she co-operated she would be released and some of the money returned when he gets what he wants. Despite the glimmer of hope she couldn't help but think that he only told her his name because he had no intention of letting her live through this ordeal. They finished eating and drinking. She slowly raised her hands as high as she could as Mark pulled the gun on her again. After how much her face was still stinging after the first strike she was way too scared to give him a reason for a second opportunity. She also knew from watching him that the gun was loaded as she was made to stand facing the panel again. Her stomach felt heavy as she made a conscious effort to stay as still as possible. She could hear his movement behind her as he cleared up and checked everything was secure then escorted her to the passenger seat before firing up the engine and driving off.

After a short period of silence Lisa finally plucked up the courage to ask him what it was he wanted, why he was doing this. 'It's not what. It's who. My sister' replied Mark in a very serious monotone voice. It made the hairs on the back of her neck stand up for a moment. Could they be related? Was it purely a co-incidence or fate? Stranger things have happened as they say.

In reality she knew nothing about herself, the man sat next to her or her real family. She was lost, confused and feared for her life. She always prayed that one day she would hold her brother before she dies. She knew nothing about her brother, not even his name but she doubted even he could ever help her right now. Her mind was racing. She had found herself in the most strangest of predicaments. As much as she feared the purely evil excuse for a man sat next to her and wanted her freedom he needed a hostage, but he was warped enough to protect her from anymore assassination attempts in the meantime. Nothing made any sense to her.

She had finally come to terms with the situation she saw in front of her. She was ready to die at any moment. She could take no more and contemplated provoking him so he would kill her and finally put her out of her misery once and for all. She felt certain that there was no possible way that her already horrific day could get any worse.

Lisa quietly jolted in shock as Mark lost his temper and punched the steering wheel then proceeded to run his fingers through his thick, dark hair. It was sods law, as if the day had not been bad enough already, after everything else that had happened, the fuel indicator was lit indicating the camper was almost running on empty.

Fortunately for Mark a fuel station appeared in sight. She felt a lump forming in her throat as she glanced across at him in the driver's seat. 'You so much as drop one vague hint and I will kill you' he said aiming the gun at her then concealing it quickly behind him. Lisa looked down and ahead trying not to shake at all. Her face still felt like an inferno and she felt nauseous. She once again was tempted to do it deliberately for that reason. She was torn up inside. She wanted to die but she wanted to hold her brother first which might never have happened even if she lived.

Mark rolled down the window as the attendant approached. After greeting him politely he instructed him to fill it up as full as possible. The attendant got to work, completely unaware of Lisa's situation. She sat silently and still gripping the chair firmly. He squeezed every last drop out of the pipe before replacing the nozzle and approaching Mark's window. 'Right. That's one hundred and twenty seven please' said the attendant. Mark didn't seem phased by it, counting the money and handing it over. He started the engine, putting his window up as he drove off. They weren't driving long before Mark pulled into a convenience store a short while later. Nothing could have prepared her for what happened next.

For the first time since he abducted her, Lisa looked Mark directly in the eyes which triggered her first ever flashback of when she last looked her own brother in the eyes as a young child. She found it very frightening how they seemed almost identical. She sat silently in shock for a few moments as it all sank in. She was terrified. It was at that point she started to fear that Mark might be her brother. Things were about to get even worse for both of them whether they liked it or not.

They entered the store and started looking around. Mark stayed nearby, within ear shot and watching her the whole time ready to pounce at any point if he thought it necessary. Much to everyone's dismay and shock four men wearing balaclavas with guns raced through the door and forced the cashier to lock the door. She couldn't believe it. Maybe Mark deserved it but she certainly didn't, especially not TWICE in the same day. She was very rapidly and very seriously starting to lose the will to live. What on earth were the chances of having such a bad day!

It was now the armed gunmen who had the keys. They rounded everyone up and searched everyone thoroughly. All kinds of devices and any vaguely blunt instruments were taken away. It was at that point that Lisa realised that Mark had entered the store unarmed. The playing field had just been levelled. She felt a glimmer of hope grow inside her. She contemplated what her chances of escaping him now were.

Two of the men questioned the cashier about the manager with whom they had a private score to settle. The young male cashier had become a nervous wreck and wasn't able to offer any satisfactory help as he had only started working there about three weeks before. He tried to assure the men that he wasn't lying and he genuinely didn't know where the manager was or when he would be returning.

After making everyone sit on the floor in a group one of the men made an announcement. 'Nobody leaves this place or does anything at all unless we say so. All the weapons are real and we guarantee we will use them make no mistake about it' he said.

Even though there were more of them and even though they were armed, she still found Mark the most intimidating person in the premises.

'Hey don't even think about it!' shouted Mark suddenly as one of the men went to make a move on Lisa. He walked over to Mark and punched him in the face telling him to shut up. Lisa didn't know what to make of it. She was still surprised that Mark had stood up for her and thought she was better off keeping very quiet. Little did anyone know that Mark had already been eyeing up and assessing his potential opponents. She couldn't believe what he had done and she certainly couldn't understand it. In one day, he had already kidnapped her, held her against her will and made it clear he wouldn't hesitate to kill her, yet why was he making an effort to stop anyone else touching her? She felt so shaken and confused.

They started talking about what kind of stuff they found when they were searching people. Mark overheard them mention that two people were carrying a ripped in half photograph. He knew that he was one of them. He felt himself fill with anger and frustration as he contemplated the odds that this was more than a coincidence.

He slowly and suspiciously started scanning everyone and then looked back to Lisa as he spotted what looked like a concealed, aged and ripped photograph. Lisa had a feeling she was being watched. She looked at Mark out of the corner of her eye only very slightly moving her head. She felt overwhelmed with nerves but kept looking at him for a while.

The day from hell seemed to be lasting forever. Two hours had gone by. The cashier had literally just looked at his watch when the phone started ringing. They escorted him over and put it on the loud speaker. After a brief conversation he was able to convince the manager to return to the store as soon as possible. Everyone was relieved and the gunmen started becoming nervously excited.

One of the male hostages stood up and started having a go at one of his captors. It quickly escalated into a physical struggle as he was punched and kicked to the floor as the armed man pulled a knife and cut him on the face. He suffered a deep cut along his lower arm in an attempt to shield himself from another potentially lethal strike. One of the other hostages pleaded that he needed help, seeing the pain that he was clearly in. The cashier, who had barely managed to utter a word the whole time piped up and informed the leader that there was a large first aid kit under the counter. He looked around then put it on the counter for them.

The cashier asked if anyone had any medical training. He felt ashamed that he didn't have a clue what to do. Mark recognised the first aid kit and looked around. Everyone in the whole store looked completely blank as he quickly realised that he had no choice and was the only person who could help the injured man, knowing full well that he could die without treatment. He spoke up saying that he would need people to help. 'Lie him down' he said as he cautiously walked over to the counter picking up the first aid kit and returning with it.

He seemed calm and in complete control of the situation. He knelt down next to the wounded man opening the first aid kit and putting on a pair of medical gloves. He was experienced enough to know exactly what was in it and where to find everything. He could never tell when and where his training that he had received would come in useful.

The cashier grabbed bottles of water from the fridge as Mark applied pressure to the wound on his arm and got the person who was helping to take over from him. He pointed to a section of the first aid kit and told someone else to find the stitches. The injured man looked at the medical kit with confusion. Mark carefully examined the injuries and cleaned around the wound, applied the stitches to his face and put them away. Lisa was close enough to hear and see everything that was happening. She couldn't process that this was the same man who had been threatening to kill her, now working to help a wounded stranger. His face looked tidy but they all wondered about what Mark would do about the wound on his arm.

'They're no good. It's too deep. It wouldn't work' he said. Mark was the only one who was not shocked and horrified at the thought when he told them he was going to stitch his arm by hand. He looked at the cashier. 'You had travel sewing kits, get me one now' he said. The cashier nervously ran and retrieved two different travel sewing kits and brought them to Mark. He had a quick look and told him to open both of them as he was cleaning and disinfecting the wound. 'The more you move the more it will hurt, so save us both some time' he told the man as he got everything ready to start with a slightly angry tone to his voice. It took Mark around twenty minutes to do the precision stitches needed on his arm. His hands were steady and his concentration exemplary. He did the last few stitches and ended off.

He placed a large dressing pad over the area he had just stitched and bandaged tightly over it. He carefully took off and discarded his blood stained gloves. Everyone, including Lisa and the armed robbers couldn't help but be amazed and impressed.

It was the first time she saw any form of act of kindness from him. He took his blood pressure and pulse and wrote it down then told them to cover him up. He stood up telling them that he couldn't be moved and he had done all he could.

Mark walked over and stood next to Lisa. Their hands touched slightly and they both got a sudden flashback. It made them both nervous. They looked at each other uncomfortably as they both got an odd feeling in their stomach. Just at that moment the store manager was spotted pulling in. One of the robbers walked over and grabbed Mark. He started to put up a fight whilst walking until they threatened to kill Lisa. Mark still didn't know for certain if this woman was his sister or not but as far as he was concerned at that moment his main priority was saving as many lives as possible inside the shop.

He exited the shop using Mark as a human shield. The manager was surprised and filled with disbelief to see them there. 'We don't need to tell you why' said the man. 'You wouldn't?' the manager said nervously. 'Oh believe me I would' replied the man pointing the gun at Mark. No one was supposed to have ever got hurt, it was at that point that he realised that he was in way over his head.

'I told you to leave my business out of it' 'Oh this is just the beginning; we got a score to settle with you'. 'With me not my business, it's completely legitimate and you know it' the manager replied in an angry and nervous tone. The gunman warned the manager that he knew from the start what they would be capable of if he double crossed them. Mark was beginning to wonder exactly what it was that the manager had got himself mixed up in. They all re-entered the shop after a short conversation, with the manager leading. The doors were swiftly locked behind them.

The manager walked around the shop in disbelief. His heart sank when he spotted the wounded hostage. One of the men stood guard by the door to make sure Mark didn't go anywhere. The other man watched over as the manager opened the safe and loaded some money into a bag. The men unlocked the door and exited the shop using Mark as a human shield again before running and getting in their car and driving off at high speed.

'We ever meet again, your luck is up' said Mark as he walked away. Although no one else was aware of it, if it wasn't essential to make sure he didn't draw attention to himself he would be surrounded by dead and severely injured bodies.

Lisa cautiously looked out the window and noticed neither Mark nor the camper van was in sight. She stepped outside the shop and smiled as she took a breath looking around. She thought she was free. Little did she know that Mark was currently, silently sneaking up behind her.

He grabbed her quickly putting his hand tightly over her mouth to stop anyone hear her trying to scream and shout as he dragged her back into the camper. She panicked and struggled viciously but to no effect. His grip was firm. He was far too strong for her.

Inside, she felt sick as he threw her through the door. She grimaced in pain as she felt her back and head smash against the interior wall. They started shouting at each other as they broke out into an argument. 'Hey. I've been real good to you up to now. Don't push your luck' he roared as he pointed at her. 'You're still alive and walking. You're damn lucky you're not six feet under with broken bones. You haven't seen me nasty yet and you really don't want to' he went on to shout whilst not letting her get a complete word in edge ways.

Something inside Lisa had finally snapped and she stood up to him and told him to move. She threw a punch at him when he refused. His reactions were lightning fast. 'Are you that stupid that you thought you could win against me?!' he said as he caught her fist tightly. 'You bastard, you're hurting me' she screamed at him. Lisa started going mad trying to hit him with both hands. He grabbed her wrists tightly until she calmed down. She was breathing heavily and crying when they both had a flashback. He threw her on the floor. He fired up the engine and sped off furiously as Lisa was thrown around in the back by his driving before pulling into stop at the first lay-by he got to.

Chapter 5

He turned off the engine and swiftly returned to question her, pulling her to her feet by her hair as she screamed and tried to rip his hand off. He demanded to know why she was carrying a defaced photograph. She couldn't believe what she was hearing and took offence. 'That's my business' she said. 'Tell me' insisted Mark as he grabbed her clothing and raised his arm ready to strike her with another ferocious back hand. She stepped back quickly putting her arms up to her face. 'Alright, alright' she said as she tried to release her clothing but gave up trying when she realised he wasn't going to let go or lower his arm and continued. 'I was told by a dying woman I had a brother. It's the only clue I've got' she said.

He stared at her for a moment trying to judge whether he thought there was a possibility that she might be lying before lowering his arm and letting go of her. He reached into his pocket. They both produced their halves of the photograph that matched without a doubt.

She wandered if she was facing a sick psycho who had killed her brother. It broke her heart. She really didn't want to believe it. The atmosphere became so tense you could have cut it with a knife. A few more questions led to a frightening and unexpected turn in their whole situation. They both stepped back in shock with a deadly silence filling the air as they realised they were in fact brother and sister.

Mark was nothing like what she was expecting to find if at all yet here he was, confirmed that she had found her long lost brother. He put the gun aside. For the first time Lisa wasn't the only one who felt sick to the stomach with shock.

Mark explained to Lisa how he faked his own death in an attempt to make people back off and how he was willing to do anything to find her because of how much she meant to him. It chilled her to the bone. This was not the same man she had come to know. He held out his hand. Lisa couldn't believe what she was doing after everything that had happened. She nervously hesitated for a moment then shook hands with him as they both smiled briefly.

She felt a lump in her throat as she was filling with emotion. 'You're very much alive. Of all the people I never expected it to be you, I can't believe it' she said overwhelmed with tears streaming down her face. She couldn't get the dying woman's words out of her head about how she would never be safe unless she found him, she felt so mixed up, she'd had nothing but feelings of hatred towards him for what he had put her through. Mark gently held her hands as she stood there shaking and asked if she was alright. She couldn't believe her eyes as she saw a whole new side to him, not only was he being gentle for the first time but she also saw a vulnerable side to him as she spotted his eyes starting to swell with tears. He took a deep breath and composed himself. For the first time since his childhood he looked so contented, like a huge burden had just been lifted.

He explained that the reason that people had been trying to kill them was because of what they may be due to inherit. He put his hands on her shoulders. 'All we have to do is stick together OK. Don't worry, nobody will touch you. I promise I won't let anything happen to you' he reassured her.

His words seemed rather ironic after their previous experiences. He put his arms around her and hugged her briefly smiling. She had never felt so vulnerable. It felt both very right and very wrong at the same time. 'Come on we need to get out of here' he said as they jumped in the front seats. In some ways finding her brother was a big weight off her mind. She was very mixed up, feeling angry, happy and nervous. She didn't want to admit it, but in reality she didn't know how much she could bring herself to trust him.

After about a fifty minute drive they took the opportunity to grab a bite to eat and buy some nightwear and day to day clothes for their long journey ahead, wherever that may lead them. After all they certainly weren't short of an almost endless supply of money.

They found a nice hotel and Mark got a room with two single beds for the night. They had opted for an early night after the very stressful, long and eventful day they had both just had. It was a big adjustment and still felt very strange. Lisa felt exhausted as she climbed into bed and led down as Mark tucked her in, just as he used to do when they were kids. He climbed into his bed and turned out the light after saying good night with a big smile on his face.

Whilst asleep, Mark got another flashback of when they were kids. It didn't happen too often anymore but he had become used to it. It had become a way of life for him. But he wasn't alone in the experience. It was the early hours of the morning when Mark woke up. He looked across and saw Lisa in distress and climbed out to gently wake her up. 'I remember everything' she said panting and crying hysterically. He sat on the bed with her gently holding her in his arms. 'Don't worry, it's ok, I'm here' he said touching her face, trying to calm her down. 'I promise, everything's gonna work out, trust me, it's gonna be alright' he went on to assure her. She smiled briefly, taking deep breaths trying to calm herself down.

Mark and Lisa hugged. He sat next to her for a while whilst gently caressing her hair out of her eyes until she calmed down before he jumped back into his bed.

After enjoying a day of dancing and games in the sun at a local festival they finished things off with a restaurant meal. They laughed about the fun they had. It was nice for both of them to get a chance to relax and switch off for a change. It was a welcome break from all the doom and gloom and distraction to the further trials and tribulations they would now be faced with. Mark mentioned over dinner how he was determined to get the family back together. She felt butterflies in her stomach for a moment, at the thought of him being able to introduce her to her real parents.

Night had fallen. All was calm as they glanced up at the stars. They led on top of the camper. Mark led contented with his arms around her throwing a blanket over them as it got a little nippy. They looked into each other's eyes and smiled. Finally having his sister back filled Mark with intense pleasure. A large piece that had been missing from his life had just been replaced. The only thing missing now was his parents and he knew that they would not be far behind so to speak.

They went for a walk through the local town the next morning. Lisa was still curious and asked Mark about how he knew what to do back in the store, how he gained his medical training. She even wondered if he was a doctor. His reply was simply 'not exactly. I'll tell you later'. He had a mysterious undertone to his voice as he said it. She couldn't even read anything in his eyes. She smiled at him, shaking her head as they carried on walking.

They had no idea that things were about to kick off as they sat in a bar. It's time to get back on track. I'll be back in a minute' he said putting his hand on her shoulder briefly as he walked off. 'Hey cute thing' said a sleazy man from another table walking over. Instead of making a scene she calmly and sternly told him to go away' as she walked over to the bar but he followed, talking to her. 'Hey bitch' he said as he grabbed her wrist. 'Take a hike' she replied loudly, trying to break free, knowing that there was a good possibility that her brother would hear her and come to help.

She believed as two police officers walked over that they were going to do something. She felt enraged with anger and disbelief as they stood there speaking to him instead of helping. She couldn't believe what she was about to do and shouted for Mark. He saw what was happening and went across. It amazed her. Even after everything that had happened the only person making any effort to get her out of trouble was her brother. He got there just as Leon said 'you won't do a thing' to the police. 'But I will' said Mark as he started applying pressure to his air waves whilst unhinging his fingers from Lisa's wrist. Lisa carefully got out of the way as quickly as she could.

Despite being dwarfed, Leon threw the first punch at Mark. He quickly and successfully blocked everything he threw at him. His opponent became more and more enraged as Mark appeared to be completely calm and taking it all in his stride. Even getting hit didn't convince him to change his persona. Lisa watched on with a mixture of shock and admiration. He got lucky or so he thought as he tripped him up and managed to get Mark in a head lock in his right arm down by his hips. Lisa instantly expected Mark to attack the man's sensitive parts.

He looked to the left as he pulled down firmly on the arm to release his airways. Very quickly the tables were once again turned as he stepped forward with his right foot whilst simultaneously standing up and firmly pinching his hamstring muscle. Mark smiled briefly as Leon yelped in pain. He unravelled his arm and restrained it down in front of him with a punch by the elbow joint as he once again stepped forward and finished him off with a punch to the face and a knee to the chest before launching him across the room. 'No one touches my sister' he said pointing at him on the floor in a heap. Mark's reflexes were like lightening, he didn't know what hit him. They held each other close as one of the officers picked Leon up and removed him from the bar. The other officer walked over to ask if Mark and Lisa were alright. Little was anyone inside currently aware that Leon and the other officer were in fact working together.

As the three of them sat down at a table Mark was very insistent that he be given a pen and paper immediately. Although sounding very strange, after what he had just witnessed, the young officer found him highly intimidating and complied to try and keep the peace. Mark started writing. The officer who had identified himself as Gareth Roberts was set back by Mark being bossy and telling him that he was going to make a phone call, he tried to maintain a strong and confident front. He handed Gareth the note as PC Jenkins walked up.

Gareth got up. 'Where are you going?' Jenkins asked. 'To make an urgent phone call' said Gareth as he walked over to the phone. 'I can't believe I'm doing this' he thought to himself.

A secretary knocked on the door and poked her head into an office. She apologised for disturbing the gentleman and walked in closing the door behind her and informed her employer that he had a phone call from PC Roberts requesting to speak to him. The gentleman in the office who was named John didn't recognise the name, he looked a little confused as he sat there racking his brains trying desperately to make a link but couldn't.

'He says that he was told by a guy named Mark he had to give you an important message' she told him. Mark was a name he did recognise. The prospect excited him and he took the call as his secretary walked out closing the door behind her again. 'I will be there as soon as I can. Look after them. I don't care what it takes, don't let anything happen to them or your job is on the line' he replied to Gareth. 'What the hell is going on?' Gareth said to himself as he hung up the phone and started walking back. He sat down at the table with them. Lisa rested her head on Mark's shoulder as he put his arm around her.

Gareth tactfully got rid of his associate as requested (or more like ordered) during the phone call. Back at the office, John, although one day expected, couldn't believe what had just happened. Hearing from Mark still seemed a bit of a shock to the system. His secretary told him not to worry and said she would cover for him whilst out of the office. John's secretary also had ties with the underground military group. It's one of the reasons she worked for him, it was a safe link between each other. 'Great. I'll drop back in later' he said as he left. John couldn't help but think about everything that Mark had been through in his life and what they could now potentially face as a result, but however bad things may get, it was still a good thing. He pulled in at speed and entered the bar.

Mark spotted him as he walked in and went across to meet him. John was relieved. It really was Mark and he was looking well. John and Mark hugged almost as if they were long lost brothers as they greeted each other. 'I've got someone to introduce you to' Mark said as Lisa and Gareth walked over. Mark held out his hand and put his arm around her as he introduced Lisa. Gareth introduced himself and shook hands with John. 'Right, let's go' said John.

John, Mark, Lisa and Gareth swiftly left the bar and went and sat around the table in Mark's camper to ensure they could discuss the next plan of action in private. Mark ensured that he sat Lisa on his inside so that he could adequately protect her if necessary. Although he didn't have a problem with John, Gareth was unknown to him and when it came to family, Mark was extremely protective.

Gareth had no idea what he had just got himself mixed up in. They finally concluded they would all meet at a nearby park in the town at about one o clock the next day and go from there. He didn't realise it but Gareth was about to start a journey which would transform him from a sometimes vulnerable to a powerful and confident young man. He could tell this event was going to change his life whether he wanted it or not. It was happening fast and beyond his control. 'It's great seeing you both OK, I'll get straight to work as soon as I get back' said John. 'I appreciate it' replied Mark. Gareth had no chance. Lisa knew what was going on and she was still quite confused. All he knew was his job was at risk if he didn't do what John told him to do and his job meant a lot to him.

Gareth and John stood outside talking to Mark and Lisa who were now sat in the front seats. They bid each other farewell. John waited for Mark to drive off before telling Gareth 'whatever you do don't discuss any of this with anyone, especially your colleagues. Meet up as planned tomorrow. I will speak to your boss when I get back, clear everything up. I'll see you tomorrow. Be careful' John got in his car and drove off. Gareth was speechless and a little overwhelmed by it all as he started on the long walk back to the station.

Gareth avoided eye contact with any of his colleagues when he finally arrived back. He was summoned over to the front desk to receive a message as he walked through the front door of the station. The message was telling him he was to proceed to his superior's office on his return without delay. He had half expected it. He made his way to the office indicated. He knocked on the door and entered upon which he was questioned to confirm who he was. As they sat down he was told he had just come off the phone. 'This comes from high up. Until further notice you are removed from all other duties and cases and will report directly to John as requested. You will discuss nothing with your colleagues about what happened today.

He has personally requested that you work for him. A lot of the details were classified and this could make or break your career lad, make me proud' he said.

John really had come through with what he was told. 'Thank you sir, I will do my best' replied Gareth as he was handed an address to report to. 'Good luck' he told Gareth as they shook hands before he walked out of the office closing the door behind him. From now on he was put on special assignment.

Chapter 6

A couple of days later as Lisa and Mark walked through the town they had no idea that all the previous fun and games they had encountered were about to kick off again. The short stint of smooth and plain sailing would now be over.

As much as she tried to hide it, he could tell she was upset about something. Mark asked Lisa why she seemed uncomfortable. As nice a day as it was she couldn't put aside the nasty feeling that they had a stalker watching them. 'Ah, I'm not gonna lie to you. It's possible but try to be as natural as possible, don't let anyone see it getting to you. Hey besides I'm here with you' he told her. He hoped it wasn't true but suspected that it was. Deep down he knew things would soon kick off again. He knew it was just a matter of time. It didn't take him by surprise though.

Things were about to start getting dangerous again. Lisa screamed and they both ducked as shots that were aiming for them missed and hit objects right next to them. Lisa's heart was racing. Mark shielded Lisa on the floor as he looked around and spotted the shooters. He grabbed Lisa's hand as they started running. Being in the middle of a gunfight was not something that Lisa or any normal person had any experience in. In fact she had no experience in being around guns before she met Mark. All she could do was just put her life and all her trust in her brother and stay near to him regardless of how scared she was.

Meanwhile in another part of town a group of four large built men were sat around a coffee table. 'Did you hear that?' asked one. They knew someone was under fire. 'Let's go' said Ethan as they all stood up and left the table, picking up the pace as they left.

Lisa and Mark were still running, holding hands with the gunmen in pursuit. Lisa screamed. 'Mark I think they're gaining' she said panting. Mark told her not to stop or look back. He smiled with relief as two men appeared from around the corner and started firing. 'Great, come on' he said as they headed straight for them. It didn't take long for Lisa to realise that Mark may have known them. Before she knew it one of the men chasing them got caught with a crippling shot to the arm.

They ran up and provided cover for Lisa and Mark as they ran behind and round the corner. They saw a van speed up and stop by them with an open sliding back door being told to get in. Mark got Lisa in first and then jumped in behind her. The two other men stopped shooting, jumped in and closed the door as they sped off. 'Well, well, well, Mark it's been a while' said Ethan. Another man said how great it was to see him again. Fortunately they appeared to have lost the gunmen for definite. He hugged Lisa as she clearly looked in shock. Mark was beaming from ear to ear for a good five minutes as he got his breath back.

After a short drive at high speed, they arrived at a patch of private beach with various military tents. Mark helped Lisa out of the van and introduced her to Paul, Jason, Rob and Ethan and introduced Lisa. 'Lisa?' asked Rob curious if what he was hearing was true. 'My sister' replied Mark. Paul, Jason, Rob and Ethan felt overjoyed for them both. They walked down to the tents and met some more of the people.

Lisa wasn't quite sure what to make of it all. She felt like she was walking through a war zone. Her legs still felt slightly shaky from all the adrenaline after everything that had just happened. She couldn't help but wonder what on earth her brother was mixed up in. He seemed well known and no one seemed bothered by her or on the offensive as long as Mark was holding her hand. They walked past a large group of men who were doing some kind of martial arts training on the way to the tents. They looked vicious.

All the tents were quite dark inside with only small windows. They were just rolling all the sides up to control the amount of light they wanted from whichever direction. The different tents had all sorts in them. One was full of black clothing such as jackets and bullet proof vests, another had various guns and other types of weaponry including knives and grenades; the next one was set up with people around a table like a military control operation room working on a strategic plan of attack for something. Another had high-tech gadgets and surveillance equipment. It seemed as if the contents of the tents became more and more disturbing the more they passed. It made her feel very uneasy as she looked around.

They followed them into a larger tent. It was set up just like a cafe of some kind. It was cool inside. They sat down and food and drink were brought out for them all and they commenced to get stuck in.

She watched briefly as he spoke with Paul and Jason. Everything she had just seen had her a little overwhelmed. His previous violence she had encountered was starting to make a bit more sense even though she still didn't fully understand it. She was sure she had recognised a few of the faces she had seen on the beach. She thought she might be going mad as some were supposed to be dead and others had been labelled a terrorist.

She was scared and greatly out-numbered so kept her assumptions to herself for the time being. She was surrounded by militants, terrorists and dead people who were very much alive and kicking and her brother was one of them. After everything that happened she didn't really know who to fear the most.

'Don't forget to check it over first' said Mark as he handed Paul the keys to the camper. Paul and Jason got in the black van again and drove off heading back for the town. They got to the town and after searching briefly, found Mark's camper. They got out and grabbed the necessary equipment out of the van and commenced to scan and search the vehicle thoroughly for any kind of concealed bugs or explosive devices. After being satisfied that there was also no tracking devices and it was given the all clear Jason got in and followed Paul driving the van back to base as they were calling the private beach site at the time.

Mark looked at his watch, keeping an eye on the time as Lisa asked him what would happen with the camper that was still in town. Just as Mark informed her that someone had gone to collect it they saw it pulling up. Jason handed over his keys.

Mark decided that it was time that his little sister had a bit of toughening up, especially with what they may have to face in the very near future. Well, she didn't know it yet, but as with anything with Mark, whether she liked it or not it was going to happen. She watched him as he gathered a small group of people together and wondered what he could be scheming, but she knew she was about to find out as they all followed Mark over in her direction.

It was a sight that would put anyone on edge, the only woman in the middle of nowhere and a group of tall and very muscular men stomping directly at you. Mark called her over. She was a bit apprehensive to find out what was running through his mind. 'How about learning to fight, we'll teach you, come on' he said as he put his firmly built arm around her. Her stomach felt heavy and was turning with anxiety as they walked off.

They worked with her for hours, until she was too exhausted to carry on. It made her a little sore by the end of it. She felt so relieved when they said they were stopping for the day. Mark and his associates had a different view on learning to fight in that your opponent would resist you with as much physical strength and counter skills as possible. With their way of learning to fight if you didn't get every step of the process perfect there was no way you were ever going to achieve your objective. If you failed, it was you that was going down.

First they displayed how to fight off a frontal assault from someone trying to strangle you. It amazed her how effective it was. She watched closely as they displayed the move. She quickly realised that she had to act fast before she ran out of air and blacked out. They gave her a minute to recover before trying again. Jason started putting his hands on her throat and continued to apply pressure. This time she was ready. She reached under his arms and across the body with her right arm, firmly clutching his clothing towards the back of his neck whilst digging her knuckles into the side of his neck. She held on and quickly reached across again, this time with her left hand to grab some of his clothing. With a firm tug with her left arm downwards she felt things ease as she created a scissor action that cut his airway off. She kept it on a bit longer then, keeping him in a headlock, lowered her arms to bring him to the floor.

They swiftly moved on to teaching her the next move. She was introduced to a move called clutching feathers which she was both intrigued by and dreaded. Jason stood facing Mark and grabbed a handful of hair in his left hand. Mark moved with great fluidity. He stepped back with his left leg as he simultaneously brought his left hand up to cover Jason's hand. Clenching his fist but keeping his middle knuckle slightly raised to create a claw he slammed it into the armpit to the extent that Jason was lifted on to his tip toes. He flew into an outwards block with added torque which broke his hand free. Before he could go any further, he slammed an upwards thrust with his left palm into Jason's chin and finishing off with a right handed downward punch to his face.

She secretly hoped her lesson would end soon as they moved on to yet another move. After a few more moves she was sore and felt great relief as Mark said they were going on to the last move of the day. She got a bit apprehensive at the thought of moving into a punch aimed at her face.

In comparison it turned out to not be so bad as she got the hang of it. She stepped diagonally to the outside of the punch as it came in as she raised her arms. She launched forward sliding her inner arm under the arm that had just punched her whilst using her shoulder to pin the arm and apply a choke before taking her opponent to the ground. Although happy at the valuable things she had just learned she hid her ecstasy of it being over. She could tell she would definitely be feeling it tomorrow.

Things were starting to get to Lisa and understandably so. Mark was starting to get concerned, convinced she should definitely be eating more to keep her energy and strength up and Mark being Mark was determined to see to it. He knew that it was going to cause arguments but he had no concern about keeping her happy, his only concern was keeping her safe, well and healthy no matter what. The next morning when they were having a barbecue breakfast Lisa was looking quite unwell. She had become as pale as a ghost and had a raging temperature when Mark felt her forehead.

Almost a week had passed since the robbery and someone was about to receive a frightening surprise. Jason approached Mark informing him that he had positively identified the address of the manager of the bank he held up and when he could guarantee that he would be home.

He complimented him on his work. 'What are you going to do?' he asked Mark. He could see that sinister look in his eyes as he smiled. 'I think I'll pay the bank manager a little home visit' he said with a tone of seriousness in his voice.

There was still a whole lot at this point that Lisa didn't know about her brother and she knew nothing at all except for a few names of the people surrounding her. All she had were educated guesses.

Lisa couldn't shake the feeling that she had just spotted her brother heading for the supply tent and slowly crept over for a peak. She could hear his voice as she got closer. She cautiously approached and her heart almost stopped in shock as she looked in and saw Mark dressed all in black and loading up with weaponry. She asked him what was happening. She looked confused and her heart was pounding.

He calmly walked over to her, remaining eye contact the whole time. 'I've got a little job to do, you stay here, you'll be safe, the guys will take care of you while I'm gone' he said. 'What are you going to do?' she asked dreading the answer. 'Don't worry, it'll be OK, I'll be back in a few hours' he said. It was obvious he was not going to tell her.

Before she could say another word she became a little concerned as he told her that they needed to talk when he got back. He walked over and jumped in the passenger seat of a van that was waiting with its engine running and drove off out of sight. Her legs turned to jelly with nerves as Ethan and Jason approached on either side of her to keep a watchful eye.

She had no idea what he was going to do or what he was going to say to her when he got back and it scared her. She was eager to know what he'd say but was afraid of the answer and could feel the anxiety inside her starting to build. She prayed for the time to go quick so she could get it over and done with. In the meantime she would be alone with a beach full of large men with lethal personalities.

She couldn't help but feel uneasy even though her brother had assured her that she would be completely safe at all times. She made every effort to behave, for one, he was not around to protect her.

After some time on the road Mark and Rob were near to the home of the bank manager. They both pulled down a balaclava as they were getting closer to the location. Mark made sure all his kit was strapped on and loaded his gun ready. Neither of them were phased by any of what they were doing. It was rather normal to them. The bank manager's week was about to get a lot worse.

The events to date had already shaken the manager. He felt a strong gut feeling and became suspicious as he entered his house.

He asked if anybody was there whilst walking around very cautiously. He gave a sigh of relief as he believed he was alone and thought he was just losing the plot as a result of high levels of work related stress.

He froze in fear. 'Shut up, not a word, don't make a sound, got it' said Mark as he leapt out from behind and grabbed him putting his hand tightly over his mouth. Mark took his hand away and they were now stood facing each other. The bank manager raised his hands getting ready to beg for his life as Mark pointed the gun at him. He slowly walked to the living room and sat down as ordered. There was a masked gunman in his secure home. He didn't really feel he had a choice except for comply or die.

Mark started asking questions about his work and sarcastically asked how the staff were. 'Coping under the circumstances, how did you? Of course' replied the manager thinking it was common knowledge and nothing sinister. It wasn't until after Mark told him he seemed quite smart, that he realised that he was face to face with his robber from the bank. His heart was pounding even faster than before and the hairs on the back of his neck were standing on end. Mark told him that if he was smart enough to figure it out he would probably be smart enough to pay attention to what he was about to say.

He was intrigued at hearing that all may not be lost. The manager asked what he had to do to stand a chance of getting some of his money back. 'You are gonna drop the whole issue, the authorities will take this no further, just drop it. You are gonna act as if nothing ever happened and tell no one or else' he said.

He made it clear that he was not to tell anyone he had been there or what had been discussed. 'I will track you down. I've done it once and I can do it again, and then, I will kill you make no mistake about it' Mark sternly warned. As scared as he was of his masked visitor in his home he couldn't help but be convinced that he would remain true to every word. He set aside some of his own money to feed in if necessary to keep his branch afloat. Even if he didn't get it all, some would be covered by the insurance and whatever he could get back would be better than nothing. It would keep him in business. 'Alright, you win' he said.

They both stood up as Mark said he was leaving. He went to walk off and turned back aiming the gun at his head saying 'What are you going to do about it?' 'Nothing' the manager replied nervously. A few seconds later Mark was well gone. The manager ran round like a maniac ensuring all the doors and windows were securely locked and then sat on his bed for half an hour in fear, shaking, before finally plucking up enough courage to get a strong coffee. For that brief moment he felt blessed that he didn't have a wife and kids in his life.

Rob asked Mark how he met Lisa and how he managed to find her as they got out of the van and started walking back across the beach. 'I, ah, well' he replied. The look on his face said it all. Rob couldn't believe it; he found it all highly amusing. 'Ah man what are the chances of that happening' he said as he burst out laughing. As embarrassing as he found it Mark could also see the funny side. Rob patted him on the back. Rob couldn't stop giggling and asked whether it was the bank, the road or the shop before they figured it out. 'I expect it was a bit of a shock to the system for both of you' he said. 'You have no idea' laughed Mark. It was great, he couldn't believe it; things were getting back to normal after years of chaos.

He was amazed and believed it was Fate that had brought them together again. Lisa's emotions took over when she saw them walking back. She ran up and hugged Mark.

She still wandered where had been. He refused to give her an answer and assured her everything was alright. 'Thank god you got rid of that moustache' she said as they all started laughing. They were both concerned that Lisa wasn't looking well even though she was trying her upmost to hide it. Mark became concerned and quickly caught her as she feinted. They could tell she hadn't been eating properly. She was only out for a few seconds before starting to come round again. She kept insisting she was fine. 'No you're not' said Rob as she got another dizzy spell and he and Mark caught her as they started walking, holding her up. Mark could see she was overdoing it and decided to pick her up and carry her floppy body in his arms.

He went back to check on her as she was resting in the camper. He helped her to sit up and felt her head. He was pleased as her temperature had finally gone. 'Probably due to all of the cold water going down my throat and over my head' she said. 'Here, you need to eat, get your strength' said Mark as he started putting food and drink in her mouth. She felt bad as he looked at her and made a mild sigh of disapproval. 'You're not well enough, rest, get well, but tomorrow morning we will have to have that talk' he said. She had briefly forgotten about it but she wasn't looking forward to it.

The next day Lisa was looking and feeling much better if not a bit nauseous about what her brother wanted to discuss. He walked up taking her hand to have a talk as they headed for the camper. She could tell whatever it was he was adamant that they were going to have words. They entered the camper. She felt very uneasy as she turned around to find Rob and Jason tightly blocking her and Mark into a corner. There was no way out and certainly no way of avoiding it.

Her nerves were going crazy and felt like they were all trying to fight their way out of her skin when everyone was insisting that she should be sitting down. 'I wanted to tell you when I got back yesterday but you didn't look well enough' said Mark. Her heart started pounding as she wondered what was going on. She was about to find out a lot more about the people she was surrounded by. She took a deep breath. 'Does it have anything to do with the people who are supposed to be dead or missing? Are you hiding them?' she bravely said directly hoping that it was all in her imagination.

'You're a lot smarter than you look' said Jason smiling impressed. 'Of course she is, she's my sister, what do you expect?' replied Mark at which point everyone started laughing but the laughter very quickly faded to deadly silence and the serious atmosphere of before. Rob knew she would probably be freaked out when they told her and Mark was well aware that there was no easy way to tell her except to come straight out with it. She sat shaking and refused to believe it as Jason told her they were all part of a terrorist organisation. Mark stressed the importance of how trying to expose them would put a lot of lives including hers at risk. She couldn't and didn't want to believe what she was hearing. 'Oh my god, I can't believe this, Mark?' she said in shock and disbelief. Mark paused for a moment then looked her directly in the eyes. Her heart sank as she saw the deadly serious expression on his face. 'I'm a terrorist. I'm sorry. It's important you know the truth about us' he told her. He urged her to hear them out insisting it would help her understand.

There were three large men, including her long lost brother, who just admitted to being a terrorist blocking her in, what realistic choice did she really have but to listen. Everything that happened in the bank, praying her brother would swoop in and save her, the emotional torment and physical pain he caused her, finding out he was in fact her big brother and now he turned out to be a terrorist. Everything raced through her mind, she found it difficult to come to terms with the fact that her brother was not like she had imagined or hoped at all. Rob and Jason went on to share one of their recent experiences that Mark was involved in. They told her the story about a teenage son of a diplomat who had been kidnapped. No one would appear to be doing anything. His father had said he didn't care if it was legal or not there was no limit to the lengths he would go to in order to get his only son back safe and sound. John got to thinking that they were the perfect people to help and organised a meeting between them to see if they would take his case. Rob told her how they had non-members and people who used to be members everywhere around the world working with them.

'We tracked him down, launched a rescue mission, five days later he had his son back safe and well' Mark told her. The army and the military all had the same attitude to offer the diplomat. They couldn't find his son and wasn't willing to launch a rescue attempt saying it was too risky. It seemed to be whatever excuse they could come up with. That's where they were different; they would enter into a showdown that no one else would even consider.

The diplomat was overjoyed and eternally grateful to be told he would be re united with his son after their medical team had finished checking him over and dealing with injuries incurred during the kidnapping. They went on to explain how they worked. Mark put his arms around her as she started crying. It was a lot to try and take in. Rob and Jason went to stand outside to give them a few moments alone together. Another thought occurred to them as they chatted outside, what would happen if Tyler came back and found her? He took his life and role in the group very seriously and would start interrogating any potential recruits and any new non-members within a matter of hours. They were a little concerned as largely built grown men were scared of him and she would have to face hours alone with him. They reminded Mark to warn Lisa in advance as he appeared at the door of the camper. He agreed that it was a point well made.

Lisa calmed down after a few hours but she still felt very awkward and could no longer look at anyone in the same way again. Mark went to meet John the next day but urged Lisa to stay behind. 'Relax, I know you'll be safe, the guys will look after you' he said. If she wasn't safe with a beach full or terrorists, where was she safe?

'It appears cages have been rattled. I think they know you're both alive, just be careful, there's a lot to gain, stakes are high' John warned Mark. He couldn't believe it and gasped in amazement when John told him they were worth billions. Mark couldn't wait to get back to the beach and tell Lisa the great news, she couldn't believe it either.

Meanwhile, Joshua was sat at his office desk dressed in one of his finest suits. It can't have been good for the other person on the phone being shouted questions and abuse at. Two other smartly dressed men stood in the office whispering, wondering what was going on. 'Damn it' he shouted as he hung up the phone irately. Joshua knew he was in big trouble as he told his associates the news about Mark and Lisa being alive. 'That's not all. They found each other and now it appears it's just a matter of time before they sign the documents that will give them everything they are supposed to inherit, if something isn't done immediately we lose everything' he went on to say in a fluster.

This was very bad news for them; a new and drastic approach would have to be taken. 'There is no way I'm gonna let this happen' said Joshua with an evil vindictive look upon his face. Despite Gareth's best efforts he was finding that Joshua had his tracks incredibly well covered.

Mark hadn't by any stretch forgotten his previous concerns and was determined to ensure that Lisa was having enough to eat and keeping healthy. 'Do you ever give up?' she asked as he approached her and commenced to raise the subject. Deep down she knew the answer to that question and she was stronger than before. 'No but you're doing so much better' Mark replied sarcastically. 'I win, you eat' said Mark as Lisa started backing away.

He smiled as he started slowly counting down from five then chased after her as she ran across the beach as fast as her legs would carry her through the soft sand but Mark gained on her fast. They fell to the ground as he caught her. They got back up and broke into a fight but she was taken down almost instantly as he naturally knew every possible counter move and had far more experience than her. Paul and Ethan chuckled as they watched. 'Who do you think will win? Asked Ethan. She's giving it a good effort but definitely Mark' replied Paul. They laughed in agreement. No one else on the beach took any interest in the fight and pretended that it wasn't happening.

Lisa led on her back fighting ferociously with Mark who now had her pinned on the ground. 'Get off me' she screamed through gritted teeth. 'Looks like I win' said Mark. She kept fighting him as he slapped her across the face. Mark tried to get her to stop then slapped her a lot harder. 'I'm too strong and you know it. Don't bother trying to fight' said Mark as she got tired very quickly. He was right. She had no choice but to eventually give up. He got off her and dragged her to her feet leading her back across the beach to get some food in her.

She was filled with rage and hatred towards him.

Chapter 7

Lisa was convinced that she was being paranoid again as they walked through town one afternoon. Mark put his arm around her to try and comfort her. Two men approached them and started to cause trouble and push quickly progressed to shove. Mark and Lisa fought back against their attackers after which the men ran off. Jason pursued one of the men that he saw them fighting with. Gareth spotted another man about to leap out on Mark and Lisa. He raced over to them as fast as he could in a panic. His heart was almost pounding out of his chest from adrenalin. Another man leapt out and Mark did everything he could to stop them getting to Lisa. 'Look out' she shouted to Mark. Gareth leapt past grabbing Lisa just saving her from a strike.

Mark was knocked unconscious when he got caught by surprise while stopping another man trying to strike. They fled the scene as it started to attract attention. Another officer approached as Gareth checked on Mark, telling him an ambulance was on its way. She fought with the officer constantly who was trying to stop her getting to him. Lisa and Jason hugged as he ran up to see how they both were. He held her close, constantly surveying their surroundings to make sure that she couldn't be in danger of another attack or being snatched away from him.

Jason sat with Lisa who was worrying about Mark, in the hospital waiting room. She hadn't been able to see him yet. 'Mark is a hell of a lot tougher than he looks, than anyone knows. He's been through worst in the past he'll be fine' Jason tried to reassure her. Lisa sighed as she wandered what had been taking so long. They got up as the doctor finally approached. 'Well suppose it could have gone worse' commented Joshua. 'We definitely need more people to get to Lisa but we did manage to get a good one on Mark' replied PC Jenkins. He told him the whole Roberts family were a pain in the arse. Joshua urged the need to get to Lisa. 'Don't worry we'll get them' Jenkins replied.

Back at the hospital Lisa was finally finding out how Mark was. The doctor informed them he'd be fine except for severe concussion and was being kept in for a day or two. She felt so relieved that he was now awake most of the time. She sat at his side in a private room. Mark reached across and held her hand as he woke up. 'How's the head?' asked Lisa. 'A bit sore, very light,' he said. Lisa gently put her hand on his head. 'I'm sorry. We're gonna get through this. I promise' said Mark. He looked over at Jason. 'Look after her' he said. 'Don't worry, I'll take good care of her' he assured him. He took her by the arm as they left the room. He got her out of the hospital and safely back to the beach as swiftly as possible.

Lisa sat down alone watching the sun and the sea on an isolated part of the beach. Jason, who had been looking everywhere for her walked over and sat down beside her asking how she was. The craziness of the past few weeks was starting to take its toll on her.

A lot of what had happened to her had just really sunk in. 'I'm sorry. I know what happened all those years ago. I also know something else for definite, he fought like hell to stop them. It destroyed him. He was so determined he would do everything he possibly could to one day find you. He loves you Lisa. He cares about you more than anything in the world, more than you realise. He's devoted his life to you' said Jason.

How they met was understandably bound to put a strain on any relationship. He assured her that despite how bad it all seemed things were looking up for them.

'Come on. I'll tell you about some of the things we've done' said Jason. They got up and walked off. Jason decided it would be amusing to start winding her up by saying he could tell Gareth had a crush on her. He laughed even more as she gave him a hard slap across the arm. He stopped walking and turned to look at her. 'Joking aside, you make sure you behave yourself or you'll be disciplined' warned Jason pointing his finger at her. She sheepishly apologised to him. Hitting someone like Jason would have been dangerous had he not taken it all in good humour and promised her brother she would be safe.

That evening, Jason walked her to the camper. He had ensured that he stayed under the same roof, taking up residence in the front seat. Mark was not the only one concerned that she may go off the rails. Rob also stayed in the camper but stayed awake the whole night to keep guard. Both Rob and Jason were armed, as were the men that were stationed on all sides of the camper's exterior.

She was visibly exhausted. 'I promised Mark you will be safe at all times. The camper is surrounded, and Rob will be making sure you behave during the night' said Jason as he ordered her to retire for the night. She knew she would not win and eventually conceded. Jason had made sure she was under at least four armed guards at all times, making it clear that he was in charge. This continued for a few days.

'You guys are up to something aren't you? I can tell' she suspiciously said to Rob as they walked through town. 'Yeah you figured us out' he said. He changed the subject quickly by winding her up just as Jason had in order to buy time for their surprise they had in store for her. Rob pointed to Mark and Jason excitedly approaching. She ran up to Mark and they hugged. She felt like a huge weight had been lifted off her shoulders.

Not everyone was thrilled that Mark was back on his feet and out of hospital. Joshua was getting especially irate at the prospect he could be about to lose everything. He was a very hard man to kill. 'Hard and fast, catch them by surprise and be ready for a hell of a fight. We will succeed' insisted Jenkins. 'Let's get to work' said Joshua determined as ever, plotting to permanently rid himself of the problem that was Mark. Back at the beach Lisa spotted Mark going through items in one of the tents and walked over to find out what he was up to. 'Not much, just going through some of our equipment' he said. Lisa was curious as to what some of the items were. They had all sorts. They had microphones, speakers, alarms, camera's, and even long range tracking devices so that next time something happened they would be prepared.

Lisa naively asked if they thought they would try something again. Rob, Ethan, Paul, and Mark all told her it was pretty much a guarantee. Deep down she knew they were right. Jason's voice came over a speaker at which point Paul replied via what looked like an ordinary wrist watch.

As much as she found the concept of some of their gadgets disturbing she couldn't help but be intrigued and impressed by them. She seemed a little baffled by it all. The next day Mark, Jason, Paul, Rob and Ethan sat chatting about their situation. 'On a slightly related note, I'm sorry to have to say this but I think you need to speak to Lisa' said Paul.

Mark naturally enquired as to what. He had previously told Lisa to see them and get a bullet proof vest which he had expected to be done already. 'She won't try on the bullet proof clothing. She keeps avoiding the whole subject' Rob told him. Lisa had snapped, she almost didn't care anymore, if anything was mentioned she just refused to talk about it. They could see it in his facial expressions, he was enraged and his blood boiling.

Everyone had tried to convince her that for her safety she should have protection. Everyone except her brother that is, whose eyes were filling with fury as he heard what they had to say. 'Get it together, she will be using it' he told Ethan. 'I never said I was giving her a choice' he added. 'OK, consider it done' said Rob. He looked around to find Lisa and stormed off shouting to her. She panicked. Lisa could tell what kind of mood he was in straight away as she watched him quickly approaching. She dreaded facing him with the temper he had on him and walked off to hide pretending she couldn't hear him. She picked up the pace as she could tell he was gaining as his enraged voice seemed to drastically increase in volume. As much as she dreaded it, when Mark was in a foul mood you didn't want to be anywhere near him. She avoided looking back but realistically she knew it was only a matter of seconds before he caught up with her.

She felt her arm crush and her balance go as he grabbed her to stop her. They stood face to face as he swung her round. 'We need to talk. Now' he calmly and sternly said to her. Lisa had a moment of madness and stood up to him saying no. Without any hesitation at all, Mark struck her sharply across the face.

It took her by surprise. She was convinced that his previous violent behaviour would end when they found out they were related. It was the last thing she had expected him to do. She froze briefly in shock and pain. She could not have felt knocked down more pegs if she tried. She felt like a tortoise recoiling into her hard shell exterior. 'I never said I was giving you a choice' he screamed as he dragged her towards the camper. Rob, Paul, Jason and Ethan watched from a distance, smirking slightly. They knew there was about to be a fight and placed very high odds on Mark winning.

He slammed the camper door shut behind them. 'You bastard' shouted Lisa in agony as Mark threw her up against the side and started having a go at her. He'd thrown her that furiously that the whole camper shook, and winded her, hurting her back. For the first time in a long while, she feared the man now stood in front of her. It was at that moment that she realised she could still be intimidated by him in a heartbeat. He sarcastically asked how her memory was as she insisted it was fine. 'Really cause I distinctively remember telling you to go and speak to Rob or Paul about bullet proof clothing and you still haven't bothered to' he shouted.

She rolled her eyes slightly trying to avoid the subject. She screamed as Mark struck her across the face with a lightning fast back hander (which threw her off balance) and pinned her up against the side. 'Wear it. You have no idea of the kind of people you're dealing with. Lisa they are dangerous and they will kill you if they have to, you understand. But there won't be any need to worry, it'll all be sorted' said Mark.

Lisa got very concerned at him turning around and saying it would all be sorted and what he meant by it. He could be very persuadable. 'You decide; the easy way or the hard way. Either you use the bullet proof vest or I'm gonna make damn sure it won't be necessary. You won't be going anywhere' he warned her. He made it clear that he had no intention of giving her a choice as he came out with his ultimatum. It was simple from his point of view. If she didn't wear the bullet proof vest he would have her locked up day and night and constantly surrounded by heavily armed guards so she would be safe regardless of whether she liked it or not. He left her with only two possibilities. She could swallow her pride and do as she was told or be forcibly imprisoned by her violent brother.

'You wouldn't?' asked Lisa. She couldn't believe what she was hearing as Mark insisted he could and he would. 'Damn it Mark' she shouted at him. She was speechless as he said 'what, forget how we met? You decide'. There was no way she could ever forget how they met and knew him well enough to know that he would carry through with every threat that he made. She had no choice but to give in to him. She felt nothing but dis-contempt and venom for him at that moment.

He roughly escorted her over to Rob and Paul to make sure she didn't try and back out of it again. Mark asked Paul and Rob if they had the gear. 'Paul will get you set up. Come on' said Rob.

Mark and Rob walked off leaving Lisa with Paul to find a suitable vest. 'Keep the panic alarm separate. I don't want her having any idea about the tracking device, make sure it's long range' he told him.

After a short period of time trying on various vests they found a good fit. Paul tactfully said 'I'm sure there's a brand new one in that size with the supplies, a slightly better one. Wait here and I'll go and have a look'. He warned her not to touch anything in his absence as he walked off with the vest in his hand. Her back and especially her face were still hurting to touch where Mark had hit her. In reality he was actually going to swap it for one with a long range tracking device unknown to her implanted in it. Mark, Rob and Paul got it set up and tested before returning with it.

John and Gareth worked hard on trying to get identities of people they had solid evidence against. Gareth was frustrated that he could still not identify anyone. He handed the photos and stills over to John. A concerned look washed over his face as he flicked through. 'These people are extremely dangerous. We have to catch them. Get down to supplies immediately and get yourself kitted up with top of the range bullet proof clothing and never take it off. Tell them it'll be authorised by me, I'll phone down in advance as well' he said. His tone was deadly serious. On that note he asked no questions and walked off. John picked up the phone and called supplies for authorisation and then proceeded to phone Mark to arrange a meeting.

Lisa was trying to figure out what Mark was talking about on the phone. She felt silly and awkward sat in the middle of a crowded town concealing the fact that she was wearing heavy body armour but she was far more concerned that her brother would kill her if she tried to take it off. He hung up the phone and walked back over. Mark had arranged a rendezvous at The Bridge Hotel as soon as possible. Paul, Jason, Rob and Ethan assured Mark they would drive a circuit and make a few trips past to make sure they had no unwanted guests. He graciously thanked them for their support.

Lisa and Mark arrived at the hotel and met up with John and Gareth who had hired a room and checked it over for security reasons prior to their arrival. She felt a little less embarrassed by seeing other people wearing body armour. Gareth swiftly led the way up steps and to the room. He was concerned, he could tell that someone had been hitting Lisa but he kept quiet in case it made things worse but he did wonder what exactly her relationship with her brother was like. Deep down, he was also quite scared of Mark. John seemed un-phased and unconcerned about any of her bruising.

They sat in the hotel room. Lisa looked at Mark as John commented on the relief of everyone wearing bullet proof vests. John assured Lisa that as bad as things seemed the worst was almost over. She kept hearing it but wandered when it would actually come true.

Everyone got distracted when they heard a noise outside. Mark slowly moved closer to Lisa. 'Stay calm' he whispered as he put his hand out to signal silence as he slowly took Lisa in his arms sliding his hand firmly over her mouth. 'Outside, I thought I saw something' he whispered to everyone. Lisa felt her heart start to race. They all looked and caught a brief glimpse of a shadow and heard the sound of a gun being loaded. Fortunately they came prepared and knew that they wouldn't have to wait too long for assistance. They dove to the floor for cover as the room was filled with a quick and ferocious burst of machine gun fire. Mark held Lisa underneath him to try and shield her as much as possible. More gunshots were heard being exchanged. Whoever was outside was being drawn away from the room. They had perfect timing. It provided valuable cover and support for them.

John and Gareth crawled over and cautiously opened the door. They quickly spotted the shooters trying to escape in different directions. 'You chase him and I'll go this way' said John as he ran off. This now left Lisa and Mark alone and unarmed in the room. Gareth ran to the left after one of the shooters and dodged bullets whilst John ran to the right as the men were distracted and busy exchanging fire Rob, Paul, Jason and Ethan.

Lisa walked to the middle of the room. She backed up and called to Mark for help as two men entered the room. Mark and Lisa successfully fought back against them. He stopped the man grabbing any weapons after he took his attacker down. The two men stumbled away. He congratulated Lisa on her fighting skills. 'Ah I'm so proud of you, well done' said Mark light heartedly as he put his arm around her. She was smiling, panting and shaking in shock. She was proud of herself for how different she was before she met Mark but knew that she wasn't indestructible.

Joshua and Jenkins radioed ahead to tell the man who was waiting to act as a distraction to pounce on Mark and Lisa. They watched as everything unfolded around them from the car. The distraction appeared at the door and fired a gun. Another shot was fired and he ran away with Mark hot in pursuit leaving Lisa alone in the room and now an easy target. He had done his job perfectly. Joshua and Jenkins, who was this time in civilian clothing, watched as Mark chased their distraction in the other direction. They got out of the car and calmly headed to the room amidst all the surrounding chaos.

Paul asked John how he was doing. He was getting a little concerned at almost being out of ammo. Paul looked across at John's gun and couldn't resist. 'A little old, sorry,' he heckled. 'Better than nothing at all' he modestly replied. Only Paul could heckle and joke whilst engulfed in a gun fight. He opened a bag and handed John another loaded but newer gun and spare bullets telling him he would need them back later. Gareth's heart was pounding. He was taken back and hesitated at first when Paul handed over firearms to him, urged on by John. Paul could tell from the look on his face that he was well out of his comfort zone. He gave him brief instructions on how to use it. Paul scrummaged in a bag and handed a different looking gun to each of them. They looked at the guns, looked at each other then looked at Paul.

He explained that it fired a long range tracking device which activated on impact. 'You guys are unbelievable' said Gareth. Paul, Rob, Ethan and Jason started laughing. John didn't seem phased and just chuckled. After many years he had become used to their sometimes strange mentality. Ethan and Jason provided cover for John and Gareth to race to a new position of strength.

Back in the room Lisa cautiously approached the open door and got knocked back by Jenkins suddenly kicking her in the chest. She was in shock as she recognised him. She shouted for help. 'Shut up. Your brother can't help you now. No one can' he said as he slapped her across the face. 'You bastard' she shouted at him. He kicked her in the chest again knocking her against the wall and winding her.

With Joshua blocking the only way out of the room there was only one option, Lisa and Jenkins broke into a fist fight. Meanwhile Mark had just caught up and broke into a fight with their distraction. 'You son of a bitch' Mark shouted as he punched him repeatedly. 'You're too late' he replied laughing. Mark was enraged that he had let himself fall into a blatantly obvious trap. Everyone makes mistakes but he was better than this. Lisa tried to run from the room but Jenkins managed to grab her and hold her back. She kept fighting with him to get away as Joshua handed him a piece of cloth. She felt herself getting progressively weaker as he held the cloth tightly over her mouth which had been very heavily doused with chloroform. She felt all fight leave her just before she eventually blacked out and was carried back to their vehicle. There was no doubt about it she was not waking up for a very long time.

Mark raced back as fast as he could and ran in and out of the room shouting for Lisa. He stood staring as he found a mobile phone next to a note with his name on. 'Please god. Not again' he said panting and fearing the worst. He aimed his gun at the door ready to fire as he heard someone coming. John appeared at the door. 'I almost shot you. Sorry' Mark said apologetically and sighed as he lowered his gun. All gunfire had now ceased. He heard Paul tell John they had retreated.

Mark was petrified as he slowly walked over to the note. He picked it up and read it out loud:

'*Her fate is in your hands.*

If she comes back alive depends on you'

He stood frozen in disbelief. 'Oh god; Mark I'm sorry' said John as he placed his hand gently on his shoulder. Mark got very distraught and started kicking, throwing and punching the chairs and table. John tried his best to calm him down. He blamed himself for leaving her alone. 'Those bastards, how could I let this happen, twice' he shouted as he paced up and down furiously, close to tears. No one could find words to console or calm him down.

They tried to assure him they would do whatever it took to get her back. Despite all the chaos they had managed to get a tracking device on the get away vehicle that had taken Lisa. She was locked in a room of a large house to regain consciousness. You could argue it was a large house but it was more like a small mansion.

Mark and John walked over to Paul, Jason, Rob and Ethan at the beach. Paul and Jason were monitoring the tracking devices whilst Rob was working on the phone that had been left at the hotel. The tracking devices on both the vest and the get away vehicle were at the same location and had been stationary for the past half hour. They felt positive that with the information they had they could start planning to rescue her.

Lisa's eyes were very slowly starting to open. She felt immensely disorientated, her vision was blurred and her body weak like that of a vegetable as she started to come round. She felt odd as she tried to sit upright. She stood up and stumbled around.

For the first time since being forced to wear it by Mark she felt vulnerable and uneasy at the bullet proof vest having been removed. She tried to open the window to escape but also found it locked. There was no way out. She heard voices approaching and started walking towards the door as she heard it being unlocked. 'You bastard' she shouted as they appeared in the doorway. Joshua laughed.

Lisa lunged at Joshua to try and hit him but Jenkins grabbed her just in time. Joshua never flinched. He restrained her arms tightly to stop her moving or trying anything regardless of how much of a fight she put up against him. Joshua was amused and impressed at the fire he saw within her soul. He found it almost a turn on. He wanted transfer of ownership for all their inheritance. He was determined Lisa and Mark would not take the companies away from him. She had so much determination just like Mark and it was clear to see. 'You ever want to see him again you'd better both co-operate' said Joshua as he calmly walked out the room with Lisa frantically trying to get to him.

Three and a half hours had passed since the abduction. Everyone, especially Mark got very nervous as the phone started ringing. 'It's ready' said Ethan nodding to Mark. He took a deep breath and picked up the phone demanding her return. He tried his best to stay calm. 'Well, well, well, what do you know little Mark's all grown up and you haven't changed a bit' heckled Joshua. They both remembered each other. It was a short and brief conversation as you would imagine. 'Stay by the phone, I'll be in touch' said Joshua as he hung up the phone.

Joshua smiled. He found it amazing that they truly did love each other. Jenkins agreed that the pair of them were a pain in the arse. 'You think they're bad you should meet the parents' Joshua told him. 'You knew them?' Jenkins asked intrigued. He told him how he snatched Lisa and beat up Mark at the first ambush. 'When we left, Mark was lifeless, he should have died. Making a full recovery is the last thing any of us expected' Joshua told him. To this day he couldn't believe that Mark had the guts to squeal on them. He warned him Mark was never to be underestimated under any circumstances.

Back at the station John walked into the office to speak to Gareth who was sat down flicking through camera stills of the earlier incident at the hotel. He looked ill and shell shocked with anger and disbelief as he handed over the pictures saying they already knew them. 'I'm so sorry' said John as he looked through and spotted Jenkins with Joshua in most of the pictures. It had now become clear why they had struggled with tracing anything. Now they knew had their first solid lead.

'Don't worry, carry on as normal and don't let on that you know, let me deal with him' John told him. He knew none of it was easy for him. He told John she was definitely unconscious at the scene as they found evidence that chloroform was used. 'She didn't stand a chance' said Gareth as he sighed and shook his head. John tried to assure him that he did everything he could and urged him not to blame himself. He felt terrible for being so blind and not working it out sooner. The discovery that Joshua had inside help, who had now been identified made him sick to the stomach.

The next day Ethan, Rob and Mark looked at each other as the phone rang again. Mark picked up the phone and started talking to Joshua. 'Why should I believe anything you say? He asked provocatively. 'Because I have your sister' Joshua simply replied in a cocky tone. He demanded to speak to her. After some hesitation Joshua finally agreed. He took the phone away putting his hand over the receiver and ordered Jenkins to get her out of the room. He walked off as Joshua told Mark she was on her way.

Jenkins entered the room and walked over to Lisa. They stood face to face, like in a western stand off; as he informed her she had a call. There was a moments silence as they glared intensely into each other's eyes. He put his hand tightly around her throat. She slapped him across the face after trying to rip his hand away. He looked a little surprised as he let go and she gasped to catch her breath. She knew they needed her alive for the meantime and seriously doubted that anyone could strike as hard as her brother could. They left the room arguing and fighting with each other.

Lisa took the phone from Joshua. 'Lisa listen to me, I'm gonna get you back OK I promise, be careful' he told her. She was relieved and upset to hear Mark's voice. He didn't allow the telephone conversation to go on much longer. 'Mark I'm in' Lisa shouted as Joshua snatched the phone away. She felt her ribs crush as she was quickly and tightly grabbed by Jenkins putting his hand tightly across her chest and over her mouth to try and stop her giving anything away.

Chapter 8

Mark warned him to keep his hands off his sister. They finally arranged a face to face meeting. 'You come alone, unarmed, I spot any police, I'll kill her, I'll be in touch' he said as he hung up the phone. He picked up a knife in disbelief and held it to her throat. She stood frozen and started crying as she felt the cold, sharp blade firmly against her neck and almost digging in. She was screaming. She felt her heart pounding and her nerves going crazy. She knew it would draw blood if she moved a muscle.

'If you ever pull a stunt like that again I'm gonna cut your throat and let you die a very slow and painful death' he sternly warned. She watched as he put the knife down. Joshua nodded at Jenkins and he took her back and threw her in the room locking the door behind him. She couldn't get back to the door in time. She was locked in. She punched the door in frustration before going to sit down on a nearby chair and cry. Joshua looked at his watch smiling. He knew that John and Gareth were about to get a rather unusual delivery from him at any moment. 'I would love to be a fly on the wall when they get that package' Jenkins said with a big grin on his face impressed and highly amused at Joshua's evil genius.

John and Gareth watched as they saw a delivery man approaching. They looked at each other in confusion. No one was expecting anything and no one knew anything about it. Gareth took the package and inspected it cautiously as John signed for it. 'Well time to find out' said John as the delivery man walked away. Gareth carefully opened the package and looked inside. He couldn't believe it as he let out a big sigh of relief, shaking his head in disbelief. He pulled out a mobile phone charger. It was a very warped gesture by anyone's standard. 'They probably think it's hysterical, we'd better go and pass it on. Come on' said John in surprise and disgust. They walked off and headed to the car. Gareth couldn't understand why they had done that, what it meant? He struggled to reach a conclusion. He couldn't believe what had happened, it was unheard of. John told him it was part of a psychological tactic, a form of cruel mind game which was very typical of people like Joshua.

Jason and John walked over to Mark and Gareth who were with the phone. 'Charging?' Jason asked as he looked at the phone. 'Sarcastic delivery this morning' Gareth told him. Jason shook his head silently in disgust and confusion. They walked off following Mark into a tent with Paul and Ethan which was set up for strategic planning.

They stood around looking at photos and anything else they had managed to gather. 'All of these pictures cover most of the premises where she's being held. Not all but as much as we possibly could get without being discovered' said Paul. Him and Ethan had followed the signals on the tracking devices and gone in undercover at night with a high tech camera to get a clearer idea of the surroundings. It was a very large and isolated private estate that was unsophisticated but very heavily guarded.

Mark enquired about the security. Getting to her was going to be very tricky. Contact was kept so tightly restricted that even most of his own men couldn't get anywhere near her. 'I believe she's being held in this section here' said Ethan pointing. Everyone went silent and looked at the phone as it started ringing. Mark walked over to answer it. It was Joshua arranging finer details for a face to face meeting. He hung up the phone and walked back over telling them he was meeting at six. Gareth asked what he was going to do; although he had a feeling he already knew the answer by the look on his face. 'Whatever it takes' replied Mark without hesitation. They got hard to work planning and preparing all the necessary equipment for later on that evening.

Twenty to six had come. 'We'll give you as much as we can. The infrared sensors will tell us if she's actually with them or not' said Ethan. Mark knew that once he left the car he would be alone in the middle of nowhere but was also positive that they needed both of them alive. Gareth wished him good luck. 'Yeah I'm gonna need it' said Mark. He got in the car and drove off heading for the arranged rendezvous point.

The car had been modified so they could communicate with Mark via the radio system. He knew that he would be completely on his own once he left the car. 'She is definitely not present but we're getting a signal from the bullet proof vest at their location' Jason's voice blasted out through the radio speakers. 'I should have guessed they might pull a stunt like this' he replied with an undertone of distress in his voice. 'I'm sorry' said Jason sincerely, shaking his head. Nobody knew if she was dead or alive and it made them all very frustrated. The situation was becoming increasingly difficult.

His stomach was filled with butterflies as he stopped the car and got out. Meanwhile, back at the beach they were starting to pace up and down with concern and suspense as they wandered what was happening. 'Glad you could make it' said Joshua with a sinister smile on his face. Mark slowly walked over to them displaying a calm and confident persona even though he was trying desperately to control his temper and his heart felt as though it was trying to escape from his body.

He assured him that he had come alone. He raised his hands as all of his men including Jenkins aimed their guns at him. Joshua didn't believe him. Two men lowered their guns as they approached him and searched him thoroughly looking for any weapons, body armour or any wires. He couldn't help but be impressed with his compliance and bravery. 'Give me back my sister! What will it take?' asked Mark. He lowered his hands as they lowered their guns.

Joshua stopped talking, walked over to a van and brought back the bullet proof vest throwing it on the ground near Mark. 'I never said you could move' shouted Joshua as Mark went to pick up the vest. 'You keep your hands off my sister' warned Mark who was now feeling very frustrated. She had his charm and fiery temper which he found both quite sweet and highly amusing.

'Calm down she's still alive and kicking as we speak. Catch as many of my men as you like you'll never find her' said Joshua. Mark felt his chest ease a little at hearing she was still alive but part of him knew that there was always the possibility that everything he was saying was a lie. Little did Joshua know that Paul and Ethan had already been on his estate grounds. Mark offered money to get her back but he wasn't interested, although they did take the opportunity for an unexpected shock heckle. 'The bank gave you a fair loan, could be a good start' said Jenkins. Joshua laughed. It made him very nervous and wondered how he knew. 'The look on your face, you really thought we had no idea. Courtesy of one of our hit men who got an unexpected double whammy. It was incredibly lucky she met you' he told him. His blood boiled with disgust. He felt angry that they would have tried to kill her again that day had he not got there first and taken her hostage. She didn't deserve any of it, and she certainly didn't know why they were after her.

'It's not too late to end this' said Mark desperately. Joshua had no intention of letting Mark win as he walked over and got in a car that was about to leave. Jenkins walked over to Mark. 'You shouldn't under estimate me' he said. 'And you shouldn't be so cocky' replied Mark as he gave him an evil glare trying not to say anything else. He told Mark he would guarantee she would be dead by this time tomorrow if he made any attempt to follow them and proceeded to jump in the car with Joshua.

Except for two men keeping their guns on Mark they all got in the cars and drove off. Mark watched everyone leave. Within seconds he was alone. He waited 'til they were almost out of sight. He looked so confident but deep down it broke his heart. He picked up the vest (which was still fully intact upon closer inspection), got in the car and headed back at high speed.

Jason, Rob, Paul and Ethan watched as Mark pulled up, eager to know how it went and concerned about what kind of state of mind that he would be in. They went silent as he got out of the car with the vest in his hand. 'Is she?' asked Gareth nervously fearing the worst. 'No' replied Mark. There were sighs of relief all around. He walked up and gave the vest to Paul. 'He said nice try. We sign those papers and he loses everything. I didn't believe that we'd get her back, he's playing far too many games' said Mark. Rob knew it left only one choice, they knew exactly what it meant; they were going in.

Joshua and Jenkins went in to see Lisa when they got back. She threw a strike at Jenkins who managed to catch her fist just in time. Joshua laughed at how fast she was. Lisa snapped. She leapt at Joshua in fury but was unsuccessful. She screamed as Jenkins grabbed her very tightly twisting her arm behind her back to restrain her but still she put up a fight. 'You bastard. You're gonna regret it. You're not going to get away with it' she screamed at him. Joshua pulled out a gun and stuck it in her throat.

'Or if I wanted I could always kill you right now' he shouted. 'Unbelievable. You and Mark are so alike' he said as he lowered the gun. 'You have no idea' said Lisa through clenched teeth with an evil glare. Jenkins was rather amazed as he watched Lisa and Joshua going hammer and tongs at each other. 'My brother will come for me' said Lisa. 'I'm counting on it' replied Joshua as he walked out of the room. She fought ferociously to try and catch him. Jenkins threw her on the floor and walked out. Despite the pain she clambered to her feet and made a run for the open door but was unable to get there in time before it was closed and locked again. She sat down against the wall in pain, cradling her arm, praying for Mark.

The next day the beach was a hive of activity as the entire group were preparing to launch a rescue mission to save Lisa later that day. Everyone available would be involved. They weren't just going in, they were going in strong, fast and hard. Doing what they trained for. What they did best.

The estate where Lisa was being held was heavily surrounded by the group who were heavily armed and dressed in black from head to toe, some wearing balaclavas and all wearing bullet proof clothing awaiting instructions. 'All teams standby. All locations, silencers move in' Mark communicated. On his instruction people wearing balaclavas at the front went ahead forming a net and doing whatever was necessary to take out any men that were the most likely to spot them and raise an alarm first hence the term silencer.

Rob and Jason received reports from silencers. 'All clear' said Jason. Mark gave the order for team A to move in. Mark, Ethan and groups from every location entered the grounds to take down as many people as they could. Joshua's men realised they were surrounded and under attack and started shooting in retaliation. Now they knew their presence was definitely known it was time that they abandoned unarmed combat. Mark leapt to the floor and covered his head to dodge a spray of bullets and started firing back. 'All teams move in. Go, go, go' shouted Mark into his radio system.

Every person remaining moved in and within seconds the entire grounds resembled a war zone with fighting, bodies and shooting all over the place. Jason and Rob covered Mark as he ran to gain entrance to the main house.

Meanwhile John and Gareth were stood by a patrol car a mile away, armed and wearing bullet proof clothing. Gareth was scared. He looked sick with fear. He was pacing up and down and leaning against the car nervously. John however remained calm and seemingly un-phased. 'When it's time I'll deal with getting the cavalry in and you go on ahead' said John. Deep down he was worried that he didn't have it in him to do what might be necessary if the time came.

John answered the phone. 'I'm inside, I'm going to try and find Lisa' he said. 'Got it' said John as he hung up the phone and told Gareth to go. He got in the car and drove off as fast as he could with the lights and sirens blaring.

Joshua was confused at not being able to contact Jenkins. Mark's phone had been modified to a special frequency just as their radio systems had to ensure that they could all still communicate after the jammer had been activated rendering all and anything on Joshua's grounds that could be used for communication absolutely useless. This also greatly decreased the possibility of any remotely activated explosions. 'All communications of any kind are totally dead' Jenkins told him. Straight away he suspected that Mark had something to do with it and told him to make sure Lisa was kept closely guarded.

He ran off. 'Mark, hi, fancy meeting you here' said Joshua as he was in shock at turning around to find himself face to face with him. Joshua commented on what a hard bastard he was to kill. 'I'm your worst nightmare. Where's my sister?' asked Mark firmly with a militant look on his face. There was no doubt what so ever that Mark meant business. He knew then that he should have killed him when he had a chance all those years ago as a young boy. 'Find her yourself' he shouted. He ran off as Mark was attacked from the side knocking the gun out of his hand. After managing to beat his opponent to the ground he picked up his gun and ran off in the same direction that he last saw Joshua going.

Mark's phone rang. It was john telling him that the cavalry was on its way. He hung up the phone. He turned around and ducked quickly to avoid being hit as a man swung a lamp at him. He elbowed him in the face then proceeded to punch and kick him to the ground. He quickly picked up his gun and walked off still kicking down doors and searching every single room thoroughly in the hope of finding Lisa. Lisa and Jenkins had broken into a fight again. She had no idea what all the commotion outside was about.

Mark hit the jackpot as he kicked open the door to find Jenkins attempting to begin to strangle Lisa. He ran over and ripped him off her. 'Run' he shouted as he held him back. She ran to the door, stopped and looked back. 'I'll be fine. Go' said Mark. She ran out of the room as more police sirens were heard approaching. 'Well done, have to admit, you've got balls pulling a stunt like this' said Jenkins fighting to get away from Mark. 'You touched my sister, you're gonna pay' he said as he threw him violently against the wall. 'Really? Come on. You wouldn't hit a policeman would you?' he said naively thinking it would get him off the hook. 'I'll make an exception' said Mark as he threw a mighty punch knocking him to the floor. Jenkins grinned briefly in surprise. He got up and charged at Mark, shouting abuse at each other as they broke into a fight which sent them rolling around on the floor, destroying half the room as they went.

Lisa had no idea where she was or how to get out. There was gunfire and fights all around. Gareth spotted Lisa and ran over to her warning her to look out. She turned around and screamed as she got knocked against the wall by a man kicking her in the chest and winding her. She clutched her ribs in pain as he advanced on her.

She was up against the wall and helpless. Gareth was fighting to get to her as quickly as he could. She punched him in the face as hard as he could. She hit him with so much force that she thought for a moment that she had broken her hand it hurt that much. She never realised she had it in her to throw a strike like she had. She ducked quickly as he went to punch her in the face and missed, hitting the wall. Gareth rammed into him from the side, knocking him into a wall and knocking him out. It brought her enough time to get some space. He stood up nervously and asked if she was alright. Gareth wasn't someone that she would expect to meet in that situation.

'Come on, quick' he said as he could see how hesitant she was. 'He said to get you out of here. Let's go. Come on' he said as he grabbed Lisa to stop her running back to try and find Mark. They ran down the hall and round the corner into his brother David Roberts. 'It's OK, he's my brother, get her out of here, go with him' he said as he ran back. She felt that she couldn't leave her brother after everything that had happened and had to be forcibly stopped from going back for him.

Gareth found John and Mark in a room. Three men entered behind him and attacked them. Gareth was being bashed and thrown around like a rag doll. He was not faring well. To Mark and John the fighting came natural, they were trained and already accustomed to it and therefore fairing up much better. They kept urging Gareth to get physical and quite insistently. Eventually he blocked a strike and punched his attacker repeatedly to the floor, taking a few steps back in shock. They looked on smiling. He was learning! He was finally becoming a man in their eyes.

Something caught Mark's eye. He looked again and spotted Joshua going past carrying a bulky rucksack looking highly suspicious. John and Gareth were baffled as Mark started walking in the other direction. 'Something's not right. It's not over' he replied. John asked where he was going. 'Unfinished business' he said as he reloaded his gun. John insisted on throwing Mark a bit of extra ammunition before he went off in pursuit of him surveying his surroundings cautiously. 'Thanks' said Mark.

Mark stopped. He spotted a bomb and approached it with caution and knelt down next to it for a closer look. Amateur, he thought to himself as he studied it and quickly, calmly and confidently disarmed it. 'Freeze' shouted Mark pointing his gun at Joshua. 'Shit' he said in fear and shock as he looked at his disarmed masterpiece and looked at Mark. Being able to disarm a bomb was not something he had planned on and ran away with Mark in pursuit.

He caught up with him and led on top of him, repeatedly punching him as hard as he could. 'You haven't changed a bit except for being taller and able to hit harder' said Joshua as he saw the look of fury and fear in his eyes again. 'Take my strong advice. Stay the hell away from my family' shouted Mark. Joshua blacked out with Mark's final punch. He made his way to his feet, panting and smiling briefly, the whole time keeping his eyes on his unconscious body, ready to strike again if necessary. He waited a few moments, still panting in shock then went to find and disarm any more bombs that he could find on his way out back to Lisa.

Outside Lisa was feeling sick with anxiety as she waited for her brother. John tried to make her feel better by saying how stubborn he was. 'Besides he'd kill me if I ever let anything happen to you' said Gareth. Unknown to her, it was a conversation they had already had.

Before he could act one of Joshua's wounded men came around the corner and collided with a device. He couldn't get to the bomb he was trying to disarm in time and dove for cover. The ground beneath rumbled violently and debris flew with a deafening bang as the bomb exploded. She screamed with her ears covered as Gareth caught her from falling by holding her closely in his arms. Many fell to the ground but fortunately Lisa was far away enough that the only death's and casualties were all Joshua's men.

She felt disorientated for a few seconds. After the initial shock she quickly realised what had happened. All she could see around her were small fires, debris and thick smoke. She screamed. She felt her heart had been ripped into a million pieces as she thought she had lost everything and life was no longer worth living. She broke down in tears assuming the worst as she almost fell to the ground. Holding her up and trying to be supportive, Gareth was speechless as he tried to hide the fact that he also feared the worst at that moment.

'Amazing' said John pointing a minute or two later. Gareth managed to calm Lisa down and convinced her to look at what he was pointing at. She stood in shock as she slowly felt her heart rebuilding and the physical pain subsiding. She couldn't believe her eyes as she saw her brother appearing through a thick screen of smoke. She looked at John and looked at Mark again in disbelief. John smiled and urged her to go. Her tears were now tears of joy. She speedily walked over, dodging bodies and debris. They threw their arms around each other holding each other tightly elated with joy and relief. It was the most emotional and loving reunion either of them had experienced in a very long time and without a doubt the most emotional reunion they had ever shared with each other.

'I love you so much' were the first words out of Mark's mouth. 'I love you too, I thought I had lost you' replied Lisa emotionally. They walked over to John with their arms around each other. 'You might want to call in the bomb squad; there are explosives all over the place. I've defused a few of them but there's probably a load more scattered around' he told him. David walked off dialling a number as he knew a few people that worked in that division. Mark and Lisa went with Paul and Ethan to get them quickly back to the beach and safety.

The trip back felt rather weird. Against all of the odds she had successfully been rescued by her big brother just in the style she imagined he might to rescue her from him before they met. All the people who helped, who she owed her life to, were following them in a convoy. Her eyes went funny at one point as all she could see were flashing lights.

It seemed a little odd. They were in a convoy going one direction as a convoy of police cars were flying past in the other direction headed for a premises filled with bombs, criminals, carnage and Jenkins. John had instructed that none of the cars in the convoy leaving the premises were to be stopped and their only concern was to be the people at the location they were heading to.

She had calmed down a lot. She felt completely safe, resting in Mark's arms. The whole situation seemed almost normal to everyone else. They were tired, calm and unphased. They had accomplished exactly what they set out to do and everyone that went was safely returning with only very minor injuries if at all. It made her realise why they were so feared and just how highly skilled and good they were at their work. She briefly felt very proud of her brother and grateful to everyone for saving her life. She saw it as a great eye opener to both their mentality and their hearts.

Chapter 9

The medical team were at the ready for their arrival back at the beach. Everyone knew exactly what to do. Lisa and Mark were checked over first. As for the rest they made their way over forming two lines to wait. One line was full of people that were fine and just getting a routine check up and the other line of people were being treated for minor injuries. Some one commented on how well it all went. There was no third line. Third lines were for moderate to severe injuries. They got cleaned up after getting the all clear from one of the members of their medical team. It wasn't just Mark, but a few people that were concerned about how quiet Lisa was over dinner. They were becoming increasingly concerned about how everything had affected her mentally and unknowingly to her were all keeping a very close eye on her at all times.

Lisa was shaking and crying from the aftershock and adrenaline rush as they got ready for bed. She was scared and wouldn't let go of Mark's hand after he tucked her in. He smiled at her gently. She felt safer as he climbed into the bed with her, holding her close in his arms as he tucked them in. He tried to reassure her as much as possible. He knew that what Lisa was going through was natural. She was sound asleep within twenty minutes and slept through the night. Lisa appeared to look and feel much better as she woke up next to Mark the next morning; she even had more of an appetite.

Later on Lisa was sitting on the sand when Jason walked past and said hello to her. She looked and smiled at him with a nod silently. He took one look at her and suspected she was having difficulty dealing with everything that had happened. He walked over to Mark and whispered in his ear.

Mark went over, stopped and looked at her. He walked up and sat down beside her. 'You're upset aren't you?' Mark said bluntly. She tried to deny it insisting she was fine but failing dismally at her attempt of pulling the wool over Mark's eyes. 'Don't lie to me' he calmly said with a serious tone to his voice whilst keeping his eyes locked on her. He knew she was. She looked at him uncomfortably. 'You're impossible to lie to' she said shaking her head with frustration. Mark chuckled.

They both knew that it was pointless trying as Mark would always manage to see right through it. The pressure of everything they had been through had finally pushed her to breaking point. She was sick of living in fear for her life and always looking over her shoulder. Remembering everything that happened as a child didn't help matters either. She couldn't take any more, it seemed like things would never end. Lisa realised when the bomb went off how hard things had hit her and how scared she was. She had no idea if she was ever going to see him again and regardless of all the times she said she hated him it broke her heart. Even if she tried to deny it and may not want to have admitted it, deep down they were family and she loved him. 'You're strong. You're stronger than me. I'm not' she said. Mark put his arms around her. He re-assured her that she could cope and was a lot stronger than she realised. 'This will all be over soon. You can count on me. No matter what you do, what happens, I'll always stick by you. Soon, we can start a new life together' he assured her. He helped her to her feet and they hugged. 'We can do it' he said as they walked off holding hands.

Jason approached them to tell them John had phoned and was coming with a big surprise for them. 'All this excitement and suspense is enough to give anyone an appetite' said Mark sarcastically. Jason laughed as he could tell what argument was about to arise and already knew who was going to win. Lisa went to walk off in a different direction but was stopped by Mark quickly and firmly grabbing her arm. Her voice was filled with malice as she spoke to him resentful and provocatively. He ignored the outburst of aggression and made it clear to her that he was willing to force feed her and would just pick her up and carry her over his shoulder. She'd lost a few pounds and was adamant he wasn't going to let her make herself ill through malnutrition. Blackmail or not she knew she wouldn't win this one. Mark put his arms around her as they walked off. 'We love each other really. Come on' Mark said. Lisa looked at him without saying a word. Jason chuckled briefly as they walked off.

A little while after eating, Mark and Lisa walked towards the cars as they saw John arriving. The unimaginable had happened. He got out of the car saying he had a really big surprise for both of them. He had a giant smile on his face, happy at what he'd managed to do. They looked at him with anticipation. 'There's a car coming in a sec. They're both really excited to be meeting you' he told them. They looked at him intrigued. He went on to tell them that it was Mathew and Leandra, their parents.

They couldn't believe it. They held hands nervously as they saw the car appearing in the distance. Everyone struggled not to get emotional as they got out of the car and walked over to them. They were all in tears as they started hugging excitedly in disbelief. Leandra was on cloud nine at being able to openly hold both of her children once again. She begged them for forgiveness that she wasn't able to adequately protect them as children. Mark knew she did everything anyone could. She felt a weight lift off her shoulders as they both hugged her insisting it wasn't necessary. 'I'm proud of you' said Mathew. 'Thanks dad' replied Mark as they hugged. They had a lot of talking and work to do, catching up and getting to know the people that their unfortunate circumstances had moulded their children into but they loved them and were just glad to finally have them back in their lives.

At the station Gareth was still beating himself up about Jenkins working for Joshua. A female officer by the name of Amy approached to console him and see how he was doing. 'Don't blame yourself, he had all of us going' she said. There had been a warrant out for his arrest and Gareth was eager to know if there had been any progress in apprehending him. Everyone had been on the lookout for him. Amy smiled briefly as she told him the good news. 'They just caught him, they're bringing him in now' she told him. 'Great, he deserves it' said Gareth thrilled with the result. 'I'd better get going, I gotta help out in custody, bookings, lucky me, catch ya later' she said as she walked off with mixed emotions about how the start of her shift was about to turn out.

Lisa walked up to Mark asking what was going on. 'The guys are giving mum and dad an escort; they're meeting with the solicitor. If they go with there's less chance of anything happening' he said. Mark and Lisa decided to go round town and jumped in to hitch a ride with them.

They'd been having a good time roaming the town and were unsuspecting of any potential trouble. They were enjoying normality and loved being a family again. They spotted one of Joshua's men watching their every move. Just when they thought it was all over. They sprinted off holding hands, to try and lose them, not looking where they were going and managed to get themselves blocked in an alley; they couldn't believe it. Lisa was worried. She didn't know what they were going to do and thought this time would certainly see their demise.

'Don't worry. I have a feeling everything's going to be fine. Trust me' he said confidently as he put his arms around her. Little did she know that whilst looking around he had spotted Tyler; hiding. He knew Joshua was going to get the shock of his life after finding out about another failed attempt. Joshua had done a runner before the first shot would be fired. He found it amusing. Lisa couldn't watch and hid against Mark as one of the men raised their gun.

'Ah, son of a bitch, who the hell did that?' screamed the gunman as his gun suddenly got hit by a bullet and flew out of his hand. 'Surprise' said Tyler as he popped up and fired a round hitting the man and disappeared again. 'Whoever you are, stop hiding and face me like a man you asshole!' shouted the gunman in pain looking around desperately trying to spot him.

Lisa tightly clung to Mark. Tyler appeared behind him spinning him round and punching him to the ground with one strike. They followed Tyler and ran from the alley to safety. They entered the main street and continued to walk naturally as if nothing had happened. Mark and Tyler hugged as they greeted each other. He thanked him for his help and impeccable timing. 'Anytime, no problem, I had fun' said Tyler modestly. 'You haven't changed a bit' replied Mark smiling.

He asked how they were and commented on how well Mark was looking. 'Couldn't be better. This is my sister Lisa. Lisa this is Tyler' he said. She recognised the name and the reputation that went with it. Lisa nervously shook hands with Tyler. There was something about him that was very intimidating. She knew that Tyler was the only person that Mark, Jason, Rob or anyone for that matter was scared of. 'Are you as feisty as your brother? Asked Tyler. 'Oh yes' replied Mark light heartedly who was making every effort to keep himself tactfully positioned between Lisa and Tyler at all times. They all laughed.

Chapter 10

When they got back to the beach, everyone came out to welcome Tyler back with open arms, giving him a hero's welcome. 'You know what this means!' Rob said to Mark when Tyler was far away enough that he couldn't possibly hear anything. They both knew exactly what it meant because they had all been through the same terrifying experience. They knew they had an hour if they were lucky. Lisa was going to be made to face a long and vigorous interrogation with Tyler, one which could mean the difference between protection and death, alone and there was nothing they could do about it.

With a little help they managed to get to Lisa first and hide her in the camper before she was spotted by Tyler. 'We need to warn you about the inevitable as we told you before' said Mark. She knew straight away that they were talking about something to do with Tyler. Mark and Rob knew that the possibility of Tyler forgetting or getting distracted was never in a million years going to happen. She felt the adrenalin gushing through her body. 'I can't do this' she said. 'I know its horrifying but it's something we've all had to go through' said Rob. He told her simply to try and stay calm, don't provoke him in any way and said to try like hell not to piss him off. She wandered if she could avoid him but they told her it wouldn't make a difference. 'Just answer everything as honestly as you possibly can and don't get on the wrong side of him and you'll be fine' Rob assured her. She got the idea she would certainly know about it if she did get on the wrong side of him.

She couldn't help but wonder how long she had before the dreadful moment that he would come for her. 'You'll probably be fine for at least the next half hour and then no idea, could be today, tomorrow, anytime. Try and act natural. We'd better get the hell out of here before he catches on' said Mark nervously. As much as he hated it he thought it would be better if he was honest and open with her. Lying would be of no use to her. They quickly got out of the camper and headed towards Ethan. They hoped being hidden from main view for a while would buy as much time as possible for them.

Everyone had calmed down and were stood around chatting. Fifty minutes had passed. No one had chance to warn them as Tyler seemingly appeared out of nowhere. They knew it would mean getting in too much trouble to say something and had to reluctantly stay quiet and ensure they didn't give anything away. They knew very well that if they did then he would be guaranteed to pick up on it. Lisa and Mark were startled as Tyler walked up and appeared behind them. Ethan welcomed him back trying to keep things natural. 'Cheers' replied Tyler relaxed and chirpy. Lisa was filled with dread; she could barely bring herself to look at him.

'Lisa. Come with me' he said as she felt his iron grip painfully take hold of her wrist firmly and walked off. Her legs started shaking and her throat went tight; she couldn't say a word or get a sound out as she felt all the muscles throughout her body trying to tense up. She knew she couldn't fight him and knew if she tried it would mean getting on the wrong side of him, which she was trying desperately to avoid, but also knew exactly what she was about to have to face.

She knew she was never going to win a fight with him. She was too scared of what might happen, besides failing dismally, if she tried to break free from his grip on her and was well aware of how vital getting his approval was. She looked back at Mark in panic, hoping for a way out or some sort of assistance.

Mark went to follow but Rob and Jason quickly jumped in to stop him. 'Don't even think about it' said Jason sympathetically as they held him back. 'Shit' he said holding a fist up to his mouth as he watched them disappearing into the distance.

Mark felt physically sick as he nervously paced up and down, repeatedly looking at his watch. He felt so helpless. For Lisa it felt like the entire ordeal of facing Tyler was lasting an absolute lifetime. In reality, she had no idea of the passage of time. She was shaking, feeling sick and her throat felt as dry as a bone. She often felt her heart was pounding that hard that it would come bursting out of her chest and fly across the room at any second.

She didn't know how to answer some of his questions but he pushed and pushed her repeatedly 'til she gave him any kind of answer. It kept her on her toes when he threw in some strange curve balls and kept asking seemingly random questions with no obvious relevance to anything at all. She knew if she didn't do well Tyler would kill her and there would be nothing that Mark or anyone else could do to help, she was on her own. He even tactfully asked other questions to see if she would change any of her previous answers. She hadn't so fortunately she never got caught out. She had no idea how good or bad she was doing and was given no opportunity to stop or to think about how seemingly obscure some of the questions she was asked were.

She made a conscious effort to make sure she complied with his strict order to keep her hands on the table in plain sight at all times. He was a very difficult character to deal with and had both outstanding and extremely intimidating interrogation skills.

Mark was also a bit of a wreck as he waited, trying to stay calm. Another member by the name of Steve walked past; he took one look at Mark and wondered what was wrong. He was very understanding when he was told by someone that his sister was with Tyler. 'Ah, sorry, good luck' he said as he walked off.

Two and a half hours had passed. As bad as it sounded it was a very good sign to last that long. Lisa now knew why everyone was so scared of him. Tyler was firing that many questions quick and furious at her that she never had chance to wonder how much longer it would last. All she could do was hope that it ended soon, whether from natural or un-natural causes. She was getting to the point that she really didn't care as long as it ended.

An hour later Paul ran back round the corner saying he had good news. 'I've just seen Lisa and Tyler heading back and it looks like it may have gone well' he said. Everyone waited in anticipation. Lisa and Tyler approached Mark. He let go of Lisa's wrist as they got closer. Mark nervously asked Tyler for his verdict. He let out a sigh of relief as the outcome was good. 'Thank god. Thank you' he said as they shook hands.

'But, I'm not convinced on her mental stability so unless I say otherwise she's banned from stepping foot in any of the equipment or weaponry tents without my permission' Tyler added. Lisa had already been sternly warned by Tyler before they headed back that if she was ever caught by anyone then she would be dragged up and would have to deal with him personally. The thought of facing him angry was a very effective deterrent and she didn't like the sound of it. 'I completely understand' said Mark graciously. 'No problem. I got some more jobs to do. See you later' he said as he walked off and out of sight.

Mark and Lisa threw their arms around each other. 'I'm sorry' said Lisa as she started crying and shaking. 'No, no don't be, its OK, you did great, I'm very proud of you. It's extremely difficult' said Mark as he held her close. 'At least now you can relax. It's over and done with, you don't have to worry' said Rob smiling. She felt so relieved that it was. Jason ran off to get her a drink as Mark was calming her down.

Lisa did everything she could to try and avoid going anywhere near Tyler for at least the next two and a half hours. She could tell that he was periodically glancing over to her, keeping an eye on her. Being watched by Tyler made her feel immensely uncomfortable. It was the last thing that anyone would want. Especially when she was forced to pass the tents she was banned from to get to where she was going.

Lisa had her arms around Mark. 'I'll be back in a minute' she said as she walked off. 'Wow she's really something' commented Tyler. 'Yeah she's great' replied Mark. While Lisa wasn't around he took the opportunity to ask for Tyler's help in forming a security detail for when they took control of the businesses in question. Tyler enquired about the current security status. 'None, plus I have my suspicions about some of them so we'll have to weasel out some of the employees and that sort of thing' Mark told him. 'I look forward to it' was often a typical response from Tyler.

Even though it brought much pleasure, he was always very serious with everything that he said and did, and exceptionally good at it. He reassured Mark that he would be happy to help sort out any problems that he may encounter. He was very proud and happy for him, but in some ways disappointed he wouldn't be around for that many regular missions once he started his new way of life.

Tyler had become very fond of Mark and his abilities and not only considered him a valued member of his team but as an adopted son. 'You've done good, you're no longer the scared boy you were when we first met' said Tyler. 'Once a member, always a member, but it is great to have everything I wanted. I couldn't have done it without you' replied Mark. 'I pushed you so hard 'cause you were one of my best recruits, remember whenever you have a problem, you will never be alone and enjoy life' Tyler told him. Mark thanked him for his kind words of support and was grateful for everything he had done for him and his family over the years. Tyler greeted Lisa as she walked back. 'If we get a chance later I'll teach you how to fight' said Tyler. He had taught Mark everything he knew. 'Hey, you'd better watch out, she's getting good' Mark said to Tyler light heartedly. Mark and Tyler chuckled as she smiled very nervously.

Chapter 11

It seemed as if the epic journey they had been on was suddenly nearing the end. The next day they would be signing the final papers. They were both excited about it as Mark tucked her into bed. Amidst the excitement, thoughts still raced through her mind. Her smile faded into a serious expression. 'Joshua still hasn't been caught, what if he tries something?' she asked. It was one of her biggest concerns. Mark smiled. It was a possible scenario that he already had covered. 'Tyler's got a team together, they'll make sure nothing happens so there's nothing at all to worry about OK, trust me, relax'; he assured her. He got into his bed and turned out the light smiling contently.

The big day had come. They were naturally all a little nervous. 'Don't worry about anyone giving you any trouble, I'll deal with them, you just enjoy it' Tyler told her. She nervously smiled briefly, thanking him. She found it strange to think back on everything that had happened to her, and how much of a different person she now was. For the first time in a long time she was happy to be alive. Mark approached Lisa with open arms and they hugged. This was finally it. It was time to go. They held hands as they walked off with Tyler and climbed in to a waiting vehicle. They had butterflies in there stomach but this time it was for a good and pleasant reason which made a very welcome change.

Tyler and his team were all set. 'Here goes' said Mark smiling at Lisa. Mark, Lisa, Mathew and Leandra entered the solicitor's office. Lisa and Mark watched silently with anticipation as Mathew and Leandra signed everything they needed to first.

Meanwhile, Joshua and two of his men marched into the solicitor's building hoping desperately that they weren't too late. 'Damn it' he said frustrated as he got a shock when they entered the hallway and ran into Tyler and his men. Everyone tried to ignore it as they heard all the commotion coming from outside. Mathew commented on how it sounded like a war breaking out as he held hands with Leandra.

They were so close to having everything returned to them. Mark could tell that the commotion wasn't dying down and pulled out a walkie talkie to ask Tyler what was happening. 'It's nothing, just Joshua trying to make one pathetic last attempt. We've got it all under control' he replied into a headset. He knew he could trust Tyler and reassured everyone to carry on as normal. 'I promise you, he's not getting through Tyler, it'll be fine, carry on' Paul told them. There were sighs of relief all round. They trusted what Paul said about him not getting through and tried their best to ignore it.

The solicitor opened the relevant papers to the right pages. This was it. It was time. All that was left was for both of them to sign on the dotted line as the saying goes. The solicitor watched them sign their names then added his signature as a witness. 'Pleasure doing business with you' said the solicitor. Everyone stood up. 'All yours. M & L Plc are back in business' said the solicitor. He congratulated them as Mark and Lisa hugged. They all shook hands with the solicitor. Mark got the walkie talkie back out and told Tyler the good news.

Paul, Steve and the rest of Tyler's team literally dragged Joshua and his men out of the building kicking and screaming whilst Tyler headed towards the office informing Mark that the coast was clear and that

Joshua and his men were in the process of being handed over to the local authorities. 'I'm so proud of you. You did it' said Leandra as she hugged and kissed Mark. It led to a loving, family group hug, minus the solicitor of course.

It was a great day for them. They were a family again. Mark was officially alive again. Lisa was no longer classed as missing. Joshua would be brought to justice in the next few days. They couldn't wait to get back and celebrate. Massive partying took place later that day and on into the early hours of the morning.

A lot happened for them all over the next six months. They took many opportunities to get family portraits done, weaselled out all of the slightly or very dodgy employees at all the companies leaving only the honest and best, with a lot of help from Tyler. Lisa and Gareth had unexpectedly become closer and Mark even gained his own love interest. For the first time in their lives, things seemed to be coming together for them; fate had seen fit to give them back their future and all they deserved.

They even rescued an elderly couple (with no children) and an estate. The couple had been living in an enormous mansion complete with swimming pool and were looking to sell and move into a detached guest house but Joshua had threatened that he wanted to buy, rip out some of its magnificent features and destroy other parts of the estate. It tore them apart and they were willing to die before seeing everything they had worked so hard for destroyed by the likes of Joshua or anyone for that matter.

Mark, soon after hearing about the situation, moved in with a price slightly under what was asked with the assurance that it would be in safe hands but he didn't stop there. The couple's hearts were melted with Mark's gracious gestures. They still had access to the pool anytime they liked. They had a spare key to the mansion to come and go as they pleased. If anything needed fixing Mark got it done for them. He also had an extension built and gave them their own drive and garage. He even paid their bills which included the best quality private healthcare that money could buy. The only thing that the couple had to pay for, for the rest of their lives would be fuel, food and holidays. They even met up for meals and Mathew played golf with them on a weekly basis. It really was a dream come true for them. They found Mark's generosity overwhelming and were eternally grateful to him, his family and his associates. They came to love Mark and his family as their own.

A year later since the day that fate had first reunited Lisa with Mark they threw a big celebration. Tyler, Rob, Paul, Ethan, Jason, Steve, John, Gareth and many more were amongst those who attended. Mark walked off passing Gareth who walked up and hugged Lisa. 'Hi honey' she said draped over him grabbing his chin as he chuckled.

Mark remained true to his word. The bank manager had been that scared that he did exactly as Mark said. He shook hands as Mark gave him a bag of money back, overseen by Tyler from a distance. He ran back over shouting to Mathew and Leandra as people started gathering around an empty pool. Everyone formed a large group, even the elderly couple and charged, leaping in the pool with all their clothes on screaming and laughing. Paul and Steve helped to make sure that they got out of the pool safely. Mark helped Lisa out of the swimming pool and to her feet as he put his arms around her.

Whilst everyone had been partying little did they know that both Joshua and Jenkins had escaped from prison and had now fled into hiding. Tyler on hearing the news kept it to himself until the next morning so that it didn't spoil anyone's fun.

It really had been a remarkable journey so far. When it came to it, a bond hadn't been broken and blood really was thicker than water. It was a story of fate.

To Be Continued.....

Printed in Great Britain
by Amazon